Praise for
THE GRANDMASTER'S KING

"The humor and suspense elements are so entertaining that I read this in one setting."

- Idaho Statesman

"I highly recommend this book. And if you didn't, read #1 (*Even Dead Men Play Chess*)!"

- Author June Kramin

"A perfect read when you want a bit of action, emotion and drama."

- Indian Book Reviews

"These books are for you if you love a good 'ol adrenalin pumpin' whodunit, have outgrown the murder mysteries of Agatha Christie, but are hungry for more."

-   Alexandra Kosteniuk,
12th Women's World Chess Champion

"...worth every dinner you miss and every wink of sleep you miss in the process of reading."

- Goodreads review

Other Books by
Michael Weitz

Even Dead Men Play Chess
Till Tomorrow

www.michael-weitz.com

THE GRANDMASTER'S KING

MICHAEL WEITZ

Black Fence Books

The Grandmaster's King
By Michael Weitz
Copyright © Michael Weitz, 2015

...

...

This book is a work of fiction. While references may be made to actual places or events, the names, characters, incidents, and locations within are from the author's imagination and are not a resemblance to actual living or dead persons, businesses, or events. Any similarity is coincidental.

...

Published by Musa Publishing, December 2013
Published by Black Fence Books, April 2015

...

ISBN: 978-0692434772

Published in the United States of America
Editor: Angela Kelly

For my parents

1

☐ I emerged from the coffee shop warmed up, but winters in Seattle often meant thick gray skies and this time they were accompanied by a biblical rain that already had me struggling to remember what dry was. And it was cold. The wind picked up speed as it whipped through the downtown high-rises like a luge and slapped my face hard enough to sting.

But I had a smile on my face.

"You are never going to guess who I just talked to," I told Carla when she answered her phone. Carla Caplicki had been my best friend since high school, and I'd been dancing circles around a real relationship with her for years, something I realized was a mistake—not the relationship part, but the *avoiding* a relationship part.

"The Japanese Emperor?" she guessed.

"Uh, no."

"The British Prime Minister?"

"No."

"Some gorgeous, ridiculously rich actress?"

"No."

"Maybe you should just tell me."

"Maybe I should. Charlie Roggenbuck. Remember him?"

"Of course I do," she said.

"He's in town for the US Championship and he invited me over for a drink. Why don't you come with me and say hello? I remember the way he used to look at you."

"Oh puh-lease," she said and I know she rolled her eyes, too. "Charlie never looked at me *any* way unless it was to ask if I was going to finish eating something."

I laughed. "So you're in?"

"I'm in."

Charlie Roggenbuck was a friend from my college days at the University of Washington. I'd answered one of those ads seen on bulletin boards everywhere, the kind with the bottom cut into strips with a phone number written on each one so it could be torn off. The ad offered annotated chess lessons with a grandmaster for ten dollars. It basically meant we'd play a game and the lesson would be the teacher telling me what I had done wrong. Ten bucks didn't seem like much to get a lesson from a grandmaster so I tore off a number and gave him a call.

We met at a diner near campus. It was a mom-and-pop style place that served college students french fries slathered in melted cheese at one in the morning and was ready with a two-egg omelet, a BLT, or a decent cobb salad for a regular customer any time of day. Charlie said I'd recognize him when I got there. He was sort of right.

Grandmasters like Bobby Fischer, Tigran Petrosian, Garry Kasparov and others always wore suits. At least in the photos I'd seen of them. Of course, those pictures were usually taken at chess tournaments or exhibitions where respect for the game and your opponent was expected. Charlie Roggenbuck was at neither, and I wondered if he'd dress differently if he were at one of those events. Instead he wore an old black Rush concert t-shirt, torn and faded Levi's, and grungy white canvas deck shoes with popped stitching. His hair was the color of a brown paper sack and was curled and unkempt like a wig made of ragged strips of cloth. His eyeglasses had thick black frames, the kind that were popular in the nineteen fifties and sixties, and he had a round face with splotches of whiskers that were making an unsuccessful attempt to congregate into a beard. To call him a nerd wouldn't have fit because of the t-shirt and jeans. Nerds I knew at the time wore checkered short-sleeved dress shirts adorned with pocket protectors. Charlie looked more like a rogue scientist than a geeky intellect.

He wasn't wearing a suit, but he had a chessboard set up on the table as a kind of calling card. He was in a booth, and I slid onto the bench opposite. "Hi, I'm Ray Gordon," I said and extended my hand. "I called about the chess lesson."

He shook my hand and said, "Charlie Roggenbuck, future World Chess Champion." I raised my eyebrows at his pretentiousness but he smiled as he said it, so maybe he wasn't serious. "I'm serious about it, too," he said as if he'd read my mind. "At least that's my goal."

I nodded. "Okay. Sounds good to me."

"Are you a complete beginner or do you know your way around the board?"

"I've been playing since I was in third grade," I said.

He smiled with half of his mouth and nodded. "Okay. Ever played in a tournament?"

"Sure," I said. "Just locally though. So far."

"How'd you do?"

"Took me a while, but I've been winning a few lately."

Charlie nodded. "Good. How about we just play a few games then and we'll see what happens?"

My first lesson began at six p.m. We left the diner seven and a half hours later after eleven games of chess, three pots of coffee, twelve Cokes, six pitchers of ice water, three cheeseburgers—one for me—an acre of french fries, half a cherry pie—Charlie—and a slice of chocolate cake—me. I had no idea where the food went. He wasn't especially big, five-nine and one hundred sixty pounds, but he could eat.

I lost every game. Didn't even draw, and it all cost me over a hundred bucks.

After my tenth loss, I asked what I was doing wrong and we began to analyze each game. Charlie Roggenbuck was a Grandmaster. I was a class B player, which meant I could play a good game of chess but still had a way to go. Sort of like me being a high school ball player while he was a professional. Charlie taught me more about the royal game in that one evening than I'd learned from all of the chess books I owned at the time.

Charlie and I quickly became friends and he stopped charging me for the chess lessons. Instead, we played friendly games that frequently turned into nightlong marathons accompanied by too much coffee and deep philosophical-like discussions about why the rook needed to remain on the a6 square in a given position or why the

Sicilian was a worn-out opening used only by patzers and grade school children.

Carla met Charlie through me and we'd all go to movies, football and basketball games—that Charlie invariably compared to chess—concerts, and most of the coffee houses in Seattle.

After we all graduated, I went on to a hyper-short career with the Seattle Police Department, Carla jumped into the bureaucratic system of the King County Treasurer's Office, and Charlie moved to New York to pursue a restaurant venture with his cousin while he devoured opponents along the way to becoming a world class chess player.

Carla and I parked in a garage at ten to eight and made our way along the brightly lit but frigid streets to Seattle's Westin Hotel; two cylindrical columns rising to the challenge of the Emerald City's ethereal skyline and filled with pie-shaped rooms. In the lobby, golden light from crystal chandeliers highlighted the veins and spidery threads in the pink marble that covered the floor. A couple of restaurants inside sported famous names, and the lobby bar had a tender who could keep a glass filled while he paid all due attention to the blond pianist in the sea-green gown a spritzer shot away.

And no matter what the government established as equal opportunity laws, hotel chains everywhere always had their most beautiful employees meet customers for check-in. The Westin in Seattle was no exception, and I was glad. A stunning young woman of about twenty-six laid a smile on me from thirty feet away, and from there on she could have sold me anything. Simple as that. Hotels knew power.

I put my hands in my pockets and looked at Carla. I took in the calendar of events and credit card application forms as we approached the woman at the lobby counter. Her skin was latte-tan and her long dark hair was neatly tied in the back. She moved fluidly and looked as comfortable in her blouse, tie, and skirt as she might be in nothing at all.

I told her we were there to see a guest—Charles Roggenbuck in room 308. All we needed to know was which tower he was in. She smiled, and I had to ask her to repeat what she said.

"The south tower, escalators to our left," Carla said. This time I did see the eye roll.

I strolled along behind Carla to the escalator and glanced back at girl at the desk but she was gone. On the mezzanine level, I found the elevators and sighed, hands still in my pockets.

"Someday you'll have to actually ask a woman out, you know," Carla whispered.

"I know," I said and poked the button for the third floor. The doors swished shut and with a lurch we were on our way up. "But what if she's seeing someone?"

"You never know until you ask, Ray. Or do you already have someone in mind?"

This was a loaded question. For months, or if I wanted to be honest, years, Carla and I had wordlessly toyed with the idea of taking our solid friendship to the next level. We already did couple things — we hung out, went to movies, shared dinners, and were always there when the other needed. But there was no emotional or physical relationship, and that was because of me. Every time she inched closer to me on the couch or I felt the brush of her hand on mine, I made an excuse to get up or picked something up to block her intentions. I'd been afraid of getting close to someone ever since my parents were ripped from my life in an auto accident. It had become instinct, and even though I was drawn to Carla, it was something I had to overcome before I could build a relationship with her.

I knew Carla couldn't wait for me forever, and I had no one to blame but myself when she'd started seeing a metallurgical artist she'd met at an art show she went to with her neighbor. I never asked her on an official date in high school, college, or anytime since. Again, commitment issues.

She was right, though, and I took her question as an invitation for me to finally ask her out on a real date, complete with good-night kiss, acetylene torch-wielding artist or not.

As the elevator doors slid open and we stepped into the curved hallway, my heart tried to race me to Charlie's room and my hands, removed from my pockets while in the elevator, were shaking.

"Carla," I started.

She stopped and whirled around to face me. "Yes?"

Her smile was expectant, but I couldn't deliver. "Look," I said and pointed over her shoulder.

The door to room 308 was open a crack. I pushed it further with my toe. "Charlie?" I called. Nothing. I motioned for Carla to stay in the hallway and stepped inside. The room was dark, only a muted, sepia glow coming in the window from the streetlights below, but I saw Charlie lying on the floor near the wall on the far side of the room. His face was hidden in shadow. "Hey, this is Seattle, not New York," I said. "You have to lock your doors here." Nothing. I shot a look over my shoulders and into the corner behind the door. I was alone in the room.

Carla stepped in after me. "What's going on?" she whispered. "Isn't he here?"

"Don't touch anything," I said and pointed to where Charlie was piled on the plush carpeting.

The room was still, like a soundproof room where each sound is caught midair and not allowed to escape. I took another step and looked around again to double check that no one else was there, to see if there was anything odd but there didn't seem to be. The bed was crisp and smooth, the lamps and their shades were straight, and two suitcases were stacked near the open closet. There was nothing out of the ordinary.

Carla clutched my arm and gasped. "Is he...?"

I looked back at Charlie's body and nodded. A 9mm with the chamber jacked open was on the floor just behind him, and the acrid tang of gunpowder hung in the air. A blackened hole the size of a dime dimpled the forehead near his right temple. The other side of Charlie's head, along with a lot of what had been in it, was splattered against the wall above his body. He'd landed on the floor in a position where his eyes, murky and flat, were half open and stared at a point on the ceiling just past my shoulder. Charlie's left arm was lost somewhere under his body—which was larger since college—while his right hand was lying against his hip, slightly behind him and palm out like he was about to be handcuffed. His legs were configured like a runner in mid-stride but his feet were unnaturally angled so the toes dug into the carpet. I couldn't help but think how Charlie's body looked like a chubby marionette that had been dumped on the floor in a heap. My eyes were drawn again to the blood, the gaping hole in his head and the hard, black metal of the gun lying on the floor near the overturned chair.

I tapped 9-1-1 into my cell phone, told the operator I'd found a dead body, then went out into the hallway and threw up in a plant container.

2

☐ Charlie Roggenbuck had come to town to play in the US Chess Championship. When Seattle was chosen to be the host for the tournament, the entire city had gotten in on the chess scene with hotel specials, school assemblies, public lectures by some of the grandmasters, and local bigwig Starbucks supplied coffee to the players for free.

Twenty-four players from around the country, men and women, were vying for the title and fifty thousand dollars. Charlie had become a chess phenomenon soon after he'd graduated from the UW and had played in major tournaments all over the world ever since. I'd followed his career closely, and this was his fourth time to the US Championship tournament. He'd won it the first two years. He had been on his way to reaching his goal of World Chess Champion.

Carla and I were already out in the hall when the uniformed officers arrived and told us to stay put. Being around a dead body was creepy. It was a crouching nightmare ready to pounce when you fell asleep. But when it's a friend, it doesn't wait to jump. I hoped Charlie would blink and groan so I could offer him an aspirin or something. But the gun, the hole in his right temple, the blood and gore splattered on the floor and wall told me an aspirin just wasn't going to cut it.

"You don't think he killed himself do you?" Carla asked. She was whispering, like she had been when she'd first come into Charlie's room behind me and even though it wasn't cold in the hallway, she hugged herself as if she were outside in the icy winter air.

It certainly looked like Charlie had shot himself but it didn't make any sense. Why would he invite me over for a drink and then kill himself? Not to mention he was well on his way to reaching his goal of World Chess Champion. I shook my head, unsure of how to answer her. "Are you okay?" I asked instead.

She nodded. "I haven't seen him in years, hardly even thought about him, really. Then when I do, he's dead."

I wrapped an arm around her. "I know," I said, "it's not exactly how I expected to see him either."

Nothing more was said, and we were still leaning quietly against the wall when the detectives and forensics team arrived. I stood straight, removed my arm from around Carla, and shook my head.

At seeing me, the two plainclothes cops stopped. "What the hell are you doing here?" asked Detective John Keller. He was shorter than me, maybe five-seven or five-eight, and didn't make use of a gym. He wasn't fat, but he wouldn't be gracing the cover of a "Boys in Blue" beefcake calendar either. Another year of burgers and pizzas and he'd be buying one size up of another cheap suit off the rack to go with his collection of paisley ties. He had a face like a drink coaster; it was flat and expressionless but soaked everything up.

"I could ask you the same thing," I said.

"I'm working. What does it look like?"

"Honestly?"

He glared like a Vice Principal and pushed past me. "You haven't changed a bit," he said.

John Keller and I had been on the Seattle Police force together. For the very short time I was there, he and I had never been close. He did everything by the book with zero instinct and it made him rigid, anal, and difficult to get along with. My style of police work had been a bit looser. I liked to go with my gut, maybe throw a curveball question or two at a suspect or even a witness who I thought might know more than he was letting on. Language was my technique of choice. The super genius crooks of comic book fame just didn't exist in the real world, and it was easy to confuse a twenty-two year old murderer with a fifth grade education. For me, rules and regulations were like a chain-link fence topped with razor wire; if I pushed hard enough the fence would bend, but it wasn't something I wanted to climb over. Keller refused to even question the rules and when the opportunity came to stick it to me, he took it.

"Wait here," Keller said and stomped into Charlie's room.

His partner hesitated, and then his gaze fell on me. He was a full foot taller than me, and Carla, who was closer to the ground than all of us, had to strain her neck to look him in the eye. No doubt he shopped at the Big &

Tall store, but he was skinny and it looked like all his weight was in the clothes he wore. "You know John?" he asked in a deep voice.

Quite a detective, I thought and nodded. Seeing Keller again had soured my mood further than it already was. "We were on the force together a long time ago."

"Doesn't look like you were friends though, huh?"

"Not exactly."

"Okay," he said. "I need to look at the scene. I'll be right back." He ducked, instinctively it seemed, as he passed the threshold into the room, and I looked at Carla and shrugged. The forensics team was in the suite and bright bursts of sterile light popped irregularly as the room was photographed from wall to wall and turned the cops who walked in front of the door into silhouettes.

"So what's the story, Ray? And who's this?" John asked with a jab of his pen toward Carla. He and his partner had appeared back in the hall like a magician and his assistant following the white flash of a camera strobe.

"This is Carla Caplicki," I said with a jab of my thumb and trying out my imitation of his tough-guy but boys' choir voice. "She's a very good friend of mine. We came over about…"

"How about we start with the vic's name and your relationship to him," he deadpanned.

"Fine. The victim is Charles Roggenbuck. He was a friend of mine."

"But not a very good one?" he said looking at Carla.

I tried not to look at her, but I could tell Carla was smiling with a trace of red in her cheeks. "Wrong, *Detective*," I said.

He glared. "Just tell me how you knew him."

"We went to college here at the Dub. We were very good friends. I just haven't seen him for a while. He lives in New York now, but was here for the tournament."

John quit scribbling in his notepad. "Tournament? What tournament?"

"The US Chess Championship," said the giant. John gave his partner a look that would fell a smaller man. "Right?" he said, looking at me.

"Right," I said. "This was his fourth time."

"So he was pretty good?" John asked, his notebook now closed and his head craned back towards the room.

"Very," I said. "He was a Grandmaster, one of the best."

"Grandmaster?" John droned, looking back to me.

"There's a rating system in organized chess. Grandmaster is the highest. The best. More than an expert of the game."

"And tonight? What brought you here?"

"He called me this morning and wanted to get together for a drink. Carla knew him, too, so I invited her along."

Keller nodded, glanced up at his partner. "Big night on the town," he said and walked back into the hotel room. He was done. Bored.

The Sequoia looked down at me. "Hi," I said, extending my hand. "I'm Ray Gordon."

"Mark Peters," he said. His voice resonated from a chamber thirty feet below ground, and it felt like three of my hands could fit into one of his. I was curious to see if his teeth were stainless steel like the giant KGB agent "Jaws" from the James Bond films.

"Look, Mark," I said, "I'm an ex-cop so I know the

routine. Let's not do the John Keller bit and bore each other to death. Charlie was here for the US Chess Championship. He looked me up. Nothing strange about it. Just an old friend in town. That's it. When we got here, the door was open, and when I saw him for the first time in three years we were both speechless. Know what I mean?"

Detective Peters nodded as he finished writing in his notepad. "Well, first glance looks like a pretty cut and dried suicide. Did he sound distraught on the phone?" I shook my head. "Do you two both live in the city?" he asked. "Just in case we need to contact you."

"Yeah, up in Magnolia," I said and gave him my number and address. Carla offered up her contact information, and he told us we were free to go. I looked back in the room and blindly watched the forensic team move back and forth. I'd seen the gun on the floor; I saw the hole in his head, but suicide? Charlie Roggenbuck was on his way to becoming the first American World Chess Champion since Bobby Fischer. Suicide? Somehow I didn't think so.

3

☐ I inherited my height from my mother's side of the family. Her dad had been almost six and a half feet tall, and I made my mark at six-one. Not a giant in any respect, but I could hold my own in a game of pick-up basketball.

From my father, I received the squareness of my face, thick black hair that had a tendency to do whatever it wanted and eyes Carla once described as the color of the midnight ocean. She was going through a poetry phase at the time. My driver's license tagged my eyes as blue.

A thin scar traced the length of my left forearm, but I didn't remember how I got it. My guess is it was attached to a terrific tale of high adventure and exuberance from my youth. But whatever injury I endured must have happened just before my parent's accident, and the memories of my life before then were erased by the horrible images that crashed over me like violent waves on a beach and changed my very existence.

When I was eleven years old, my parents were killed

by a drunk driver on I-90 while they were returning home from their anniversary getaway at Salish Lodge, a rustic yet ritzy hotel perched above the thunderous Snoqualmie Falls in the Cascade Mountains. At least they had the weekend together before the drunk hit their car and sent them careening under the crushing wheels of an eighteen-wheeler.

From that day forward, my Uncle Dave had been at my side. Instead of friends, I gorged myself on television sitcoms like a leech. My high school career was a mish-mash of one-liners and gaffs. The only sanity was chess. My dad had taught me the basics of the game when I was five. I took to it because of the knights and castles, the King and Queen, the sheer mystery of the medieval times they represented to me. It's how I'd always thought of the game, a cloak and dagger battle of wits over the board.

Uncle Dave refined the game of chess for me. He introduced me to tactics like pins, knight forks, and discovered attacks; he showed me the shocking beauty of a queen sacrifice and the subtle constriction brought about by a clever battalion of pawns. He taught me how the game is really an art.

I received a massive settlement from my parents' accident. I didn't know. I was eleven and had just lost them both. Uncle Dave didn't spend a dime of the insurance money, and as long as I was careful with it, I would never have to work again if I didn't want to. I wasn't rich, but I could pay the bills. With the economy in the tank, though, I made some extra cash by teaching chess to kids and adult club players. "Keep yourself busy," Uncle Dave always said. "Don't just exist." When he was diagnosed with an inoperable cancer, I was in my twenties.

Days before he died, Uncle Dave told me I had too much money to keep to myself. "Use it to do something for someone," he said. "Either pass on a favor done for you or help someone in a way you never were."

At the time, I thought he sounded like a greeting card so I just nodded and smiled. After he was gone, though, I realized everything he'd done for me while I was growing up, so I started donating both my time and my money to the Brookstone Youth Center. It was part school, part shelter, and part hangout for those kids called "disadvantaged," which meant kids with no parents, one parent, or parents who don't care. That was one side. The kids themselves were the other side. In some cases, it was the child who had simply left home.

I taught or played chess with any of the kids, but on the day Charlie Roggenbuck had called me, I'd been working with a sixteen-year-old boy named Alex Donovan. He went by "X"; I called him Alex and he was on his way to becoming a very good chess player. He had the instincts of an attacker but also possessed the patience of a strategist. Rare for someone so young in any sport. I'd always believed chess taught us skills to use in life like patience, looking ahead before making a move, and looking at all of the options and threats. Maybe Alex's personal life had taught him how to survive on the chessboard.

Alex had basically been on his own since he was fourteen, and that's all I really knew. I was a volunteer, not a counselor, so I didn't pry. I was there to teach chess, and it was something Alex enjoyed and was good at.

"You know who that was?" I asked him when I'd

hung up with Charlie.

"Uh, no," Alex said. He was almost six feet tall and had shaggy blond hair that fell into his eyes. I liked to think of him as a California surfer-dude.

"Grandmaster Charlie Roggenbuck. Ever heard of him?"

"No way! You know The Buck?"

I smiled. "I'm not sure how he'd feel about being called 'The Buck,'" I said. "Maybe I'll ask him when I see him tonight."

At ten a.m., the morning following our discovery of Charlie's body, and after I'd called Carla to make sure she was okay, I brought my Land Cruiser to a stop outside the youth center and got out. The sky was flat and gray with more menacing clouds, dark and roiling, battling through a storm out over the Pacific. I took a deep breath of the cold salty air coming off Elliot Bay and let the previous day's conversation with Alex seep out.

Inside the youth center, I found Mary Conner, Alex's counselor. She always wore professional slacks and button-up blouses of varying hues, but her spiky, short-cropped neon orange hair and jangling bracelets made her easy to find from a distance.

"Hi, Mr. Gordon," she said when I waved to her.

"Mary, you know I've asked you to call me Ray," I said in a weak attempt to chastise her.

"I tried that once. I just can't. You know?" I nodded. No point in it really. "Alex was pretty excited after you got that call from your chess friend yesterday," she said. "He's really hoping to meet him."

"Is Alex here?" I asked.

"Yeah. He's in the game room as usual."

"Thanks."

The game room at the Brookstone Youth Center was by itself a reason for eligible teenagers to want to gain entry. It had two pool tables, two foosball tables, ten chess sets, an homage to both Parker Brothers and Milton Bradley, a small library, magazines, snack and soda vending machines, and the Seattle adolescent must, an espresso maker. Alex was sitting in a corner with a chessboard going over tactical problems from a book. He looked up when I rolled a billiard ball into a pocket and it clacked against its brethren.

"Gordo!" he said. I went over and sat across the chessboard from him. Instinctively, I reached for a rook then pulled my hand back. Alex was working the problem on the board, not me, but he didn't seem to notice. "So how's The Buck? Did he kick your ass in a game?"

"No. I'm afraid we didn't get to play," I said.

"Why not? What's up?"

"When I got there..." I said. Charlie was my friend, and it was hard enough to remind myself he was dead by his own hand, let alone tell a kid who thought the world of him.

"What?" Alex asked.

"Uh... He's dead, Alex. When I got to the hotel, Charlie was dead."

After leaving the Youth Center, I drove a few blocks

further into the city and parked in a garage downtown near the Westlake Shopping Center. The plaza outside the mall was ringed with homeless men folded into doorways and corporate types crisscrossing the square. While the destitute had wrapped themselves in layers of castaway clothes and curled up beneath the sculptures, the business types walked fast, their wool coats open to the sharp January winds, flapping for attention.

I bought a ticket on the third floor of Westlake Center and rode the Monorail, an elevated train straddling a single large track. It was built for the 1962 World's Fair to shuttle people from downtown to Seattle Center. It was a two-minute ride from the shopping district to Seattle Center and overlooked the businesses too small to afford the prime real estate downtown.

In its day, I'm sure the Monorail looked like a futuristic mode of public transportation, snaking its way overhead and fitting right in with the Space Needle to complete the Buck Rogers look. Sitting on the aquamarine colored plastic seats now, though, just brought up memories of bad nineteen sixties color schemes and that era's idea of what the future might look like.

I stared out the window as we passed the Westin Hotel, and I saw down through the glass-ceilinged restaurant where guests were having lunch, probably unaware of the man who'd been found dead in room 308. In a blink, I was looking at a parking garage, then the glowing red neon sign of a Chinese restaurant, a parking lot, a jazz bar with a band of instruments painted on the outside wall, an intersection as the Monorail passed over 7th Avenue, the Pink Elephant Car Wash, and a McDonald's, then darkness as we passed through the

Experience Music Project before coming to a halt.

The US Chess Championship consisted of nine rounds played over the course of two weeks. All twenty-four players were rated two thousand—experts—or better at the game and competed for the title and the cash prize of fifty thousand dollars. The games were being played at the Seattle Center, near the Space Needle. Now an area filled with art, theatre, museums, scientific exhibits, and an amusement park, the Seattle Center had been ground zero for the World's Fair.

That day was to have seen the fifth round of play, but out of respect for Charlie, games had been postponed. The directors also needed to reconfigure the playing schedule and during that process, I hoped to talk to as many people as I could.

As I expected, several of the players were there anyway, analyzing games, talking or playing blitz with one another. No one gets to the US Championship by sitting around and doing nothing. The room was a long rectangle with wood paneling on the walls and recessed lights that ran the length of the ceiling and gave the hall a welcome feeling of warmth. Three aisles were created by two rows of tables. On each table was a chess set, the silent armies standing resolute, facing each other from opposite sides of the board prepared for the inevitable battle.

Even though there was no forced entry into Charlie's hotel room and as far as I had seen nothing was missing, something nagged at me. Charlie wasn't alone when he died, or at least he wasn't alone all day. Yes, there was a gun near his body. Yes, it looked like a suicide. Maybe that was it, it *looked* like a suicide. What gnawed at me was that on the table next to Charlie had been a chess game in progress. Nothing could convince me he hadn't been playing someone either just before or when he died. Of course, if it wasn't suicide it had to be murder.

Most of the faces in the room were recognizable from the pages of *Chess Life* magazine, all of them the best minds in the game from all over the country. In the far corner, Vladimir Penski was staring at the board before him like a telekinetic. He was a product of the defunct Soviet Union, a former soldier of the Red Army who lived in Philadelphia and made a living as a jeweler. Just like most professional chess players, Vladimir Penski had a day job to support his chess career. Endorsement contracts for popular chess stars were neither frequent nor lucrative.

There were college students, bankers, engineers, business owners, and at least one doctor I knew of. Ron Meadows was there. I'd played him at the US Amateur West Championship in Los Angeles. Ron was a nice enough guy and an excellent chess player, but his nose whistled whenever he closed his mouth. Nobody knew if the whistling was on purpose, but it was very distracting to his opponents.

Yuri Milosevek sat at his table and leaned against the wall so he stared at his board from the corner. He was only 47 but looked old enough to be my grandfather. The nicotine from three packs of cigarettes a day had turned him into a human raisin. Yuri wore multi-colored flower-print Hawaiian shirts that were one size too small, and he talked very slowly, as if each word was assembled with agonizing effort. But his chess game was sharp. Yuri was one of the favorites to make a bid for the US Chess Championship.

Elena Johnson was a quietly attractive woman from New York. She'd won the Women's New York State Championship at age nineteen, and then vanished. Most people believed she retired, at least temporarily, from chess in order to attend college, but there were plenty of conspiracy theorists who maintained she'd been abducted by underground agents of the former Soviet Union who were trying to bring back the glory of communism. No matter what was rumored about her, when Elena resurfaced to play chess once again, it was with a vengeance by winning tournament after tournament.

I spotted Ryan Brooks sitting in a corner eating Cheetos from the bag. Ryan had been a child prodigy; winning every major chess tournament he played in through high school. He played little while attending college, but got back into the chess scene once he was an established software writer in California. More than once he'd been reprimanded for passing snack food residue from his fingers to the chess pieces and because of it he was known as "Smudge" behind his back.

I thought of Alex Donovan at the youth center. If he wasn't so down on life in general, he might turn out like Ryan. Not a chess prodigy, but he could be successful if he put his mind to it.

I recognized or knew almost every one of the players. My questions were which one could and would commit murder and why?

Vladimir Penski was first on my list to talk with. He was old enough to be Charlie's father, but they knew each other well on a chess-based social level. They'd played in hundreds of tournaments and usually ended up playing each other. Whether they liked each other or not was another matter. They'd been known to disagree, but when it came to Grandmasters, disagreement was common. Two big dogs wanting to chew the same bone in the same place and at the same time didn't usually work. "Vladimir," I said walking up to him. His eyes were watery and stained pink, but he recognized me.

"Raymond," he said, standing up from the table. We shook hands and he smiled, showing a row of teeth any dentist would find challenging. "How long has it been?" he asked, his Russian accent tinted with eastern seaboard swagger. "Three years? At the Open?"

I nodded. His memory was good. The National Open in Las Vegas was the last time I'd seen Charlie alive as well. Charlie and I, along with the former US Champion and two tournament directors, had spent our final night in Sin City blowing wads of cash at a Caesar's Palace roulette table and buying drinks for gorgeous young women who had no qualms about getting freebies from strange older men. And since we neither made any money nor developed relationships with any of the women, it was all justified as harmless fun.

Vladimir Penski was about sixty years old with a head of thick black hair that sported silver racing stripes shooting back from his temples. He carried an extra twenty pounds around his middle, and I thought the friendly look in his eye would make him an excellent candidate for a shopping mall Santa Claus someday—if he could get his Grinchified teeth fixed. We sat down and I looked over the pieces on the board between us. They were set up to match a diagram in a book lying open next to Vladimir's elbow. I wanted to move a Knight to attack.

"I'm sorry we couldn't have met under better circumstances this time," I said.

"So you've heard about Charles then," he said.

"Heard about it? I found him."

"Oh no. I'm so sorry to hear that, Raymond. It should not have been you. You were too good of friends."

I nodded. "We were going to have a drink." It made me wonder if Charlie might have had drinks with anyone else at the tournament. Why did he call me when he did, several days into the tournament instead of when he'd first arrived in Seattle? Had something happened? I watched the players scattered around the room and then said, "Vladimir, do you remember anything going on between Charlie and anyone here at the tournament the last few days?"

"Going on? Like fight?" he asked.

"Not necessarily a fight, but anything, anything out of the ordinary. Was he talking with anyone more than usual? Was he putting the moves on Miss Hayes over there?" I asked nodding toward a lovely young woman of twenty-four, who happened to be the highest ranked female player in the country. "Or, as you said, was he openly arguing with anyone?"

"Raymond," Vladimir said, his voice raspy as he whispered through the pieces on the table, "we all know you used to be police man, but you think someone here did this to Charles? We heard it was suicide."

"Why would he kill himself?" I asked. Mentally I shook my head. Suicide just didn't fit. Or maybe I just didn't want it to. "I don't know what I think right now. But I think these are the only people in Seattle, besides me, who he knew."

4

☐ I said hello to a few of the other players and after receiving the same condolences, I found one of the tournament arbiters, Graham Saunders, and asked him to join me in one of the small rooms used as offices. The walls were white and undecorated except for a faded photograph of Seattle, probably taken from Queen Anne Hill. There was a boxy, put-it-together-yourself desk under the picture with two chairs in front of it. I motioned Graham to the seat behind the desk and asked him the same questions I had asked Vladimir Penski.

"According to the story in the newspaper it was self-inflicted. The police said the gun was right there. Why would you think it was one of the chess players, Ray?" asked Saunders. He was a former US Chess Champion himself, winner of the US Open and the National Open in the nineteen eighties. He was tall and thin with wisps of faded blond hair. As the tournament arbiter, he wore a suit and tie and kept meticulous records of everything he did. The image was a good fit for him because outside the world of chess, he was an engineer with a large firm where he always wore a suit and tie and kept meticulous records of everything he did. I had never played chess with Graham, but I had talked with him outside tournament rooms. Graham Saunders knew or knew of everyone who played serious chess. "No one here is capable of such an act, Ray," he said.

I shrugged. "Everyone has a breaking point, Graham. This is the United States Chess Championship. Everyone involved is under tremendous pressure. I'm not accusing anyone of anything right now, but I just don't believe Charlie would kill himself."

"Don't believe or can't believe it?" Graham leaned forward, putting his elbows on the desk. "Ray, please forgive me if what I'm about to say offends you, but...you're no longer a police officer."

"I'm well aware of that Graham," I said. "But Charlie and I were friends and, frankly, the detective who's heading up the investigation is clueless." I shook my head, wondering if I was being fair to Keller. "I know these people," I said. "I can figure it out."

"Can you do that? I mean, legally?"

"As long as I don't interfere with the official investigation."

Graham nodded and sat back. "Well, good luck to you then."

Anna Krimpski was the other arbiter, but according to Saunders, she had taken advantage of the break in play to run some personal errands. I'd never met Ms. Krimpski, but she was said to be as cold as Siberia, as tough as her coal miner father, and as deceiving as Stalin. She'd been described this way in the United States Chess Federation's official magazine *Chess Life* many years ago, and while the journalist had been referring to her style of play on the board, those who met her hung the label around her neck as well.

The organizer of the event, Nigel Cross, was out as well, and I saw little advantage in bothering with any of the corporate sponsors. The monorail zipped me back to the shopping district where I jostled my way through the multi-level maze of shops, kiosks, and frenzied consumers in the mall. Once outside, I walked east on Olive past Bartell's Drug store then cut across to the Starbuck's on the corner of 6th and Stewart. After another couple of blocks, I'd seen enough delis and antique stores that I actually *wanted* to sit down at a Chippendale table and enjoy a submarine sandwich.

The area catered heavily to business types who worked in the glass-faced high rises that lined 6th and 7th Avenues, as well as the patrons of the many hotels, including the Westin.

Most of the pedestrian traffic walked quickly from an office building to a sandwich shop and then finished out their lunch break window shopping while knocking back a couple of espressos.

On 8th Avenue, I ducked into a dark hole in the wall called the Hideout and waited inside by the door while my eyes adjusted to the sudden loss of light.

"Hey, hey! There's our boy, Ray!" I heard a voice call.

I smiled. It was Tommy Ryder.

Tommy was a professional student at the University of Washington where he worked in medical labs conducting experiments while collecting degrees and young women. He was also what some people might call a law enforcement enthusiast. He came from a long family line of cops and was interested in everything having to do with police work. At the age of twenty-seven, he had Bachelor's degrees in criminal justice, forensic science, and sociology. He was working on a Master's degree and would probably get another Bachelor's in something else along the way.

People often asked Tommy why he wasn't a cop like everyone else in his family. The answer was always a smile, a shrug, and a quick answer. Sometimes he'd say, "I just don't have the upper body strength," or "Mom wanted at least one smart kid in the family." The truth was that as interested as he was in law enforcement, he just didn't want to be a man in uniform. He talked about cases his dad or brothers were working on, bought rounds of beer whenever one of them solved a case, but he just didn't want to follow in their shoes. "I guess I'm the black sheep of the family," he once told me. Sometimes I wondered if he was hiding out in college or if he was actually looking for a career he thought might win him some respect from his family.

"Tommy Ryder," I called back and waited for the joke.

"Ride 'er?" he said. "I don't even know 'er!"

Every time, I thought, and shook my head. I smiled and bypassed two burly guys at the bar, then sidestepped a waitress balancing a tray stacked with dirty plates and glasses. I slid into the booth opposite Tommy and looked him over. His usual white button-up and tweed sports jacket were neat and rumple free, but his black hair stood up on one side and was crushed on the other as if he'd just rolled out of bed. His right eye was blue and the left one was brown, and he often joked about putting a red contact over the brown one so his eyes would look like police flashers. "How's it going today?" I asked.

"Not bad. Kind of slow though. Not much going on in this weather," he said. "How 'bout you?"

I shrugged. "What are you having?" I asked pointing to his empty glass.

"The usual."

I motioned to Al the bartender for two more of what Tommy was drinking. He nodded and brought us a couple of glasses of orange juice with a float of Grand Marnier. It was Tommy's idea of a sophisticated screwdriver. I swirled the liqueur into the juice and took a sip.

"I painted my truck," Tommy said.

"What do you mean? I just saw it outside. Looks the same." Tommy drove an old nineteen sixties era GMC that was the identical shade of turquoise found in an elementary school bathroom.

He shook his head. "Not the body. Are you kidding? You can't find that color anymore. I painted the undercarriage. Neon orange so they'll be able to find me."

"Find you? What are you talking about?"

"Remember the story a month or so back about the couple who ran off the road up by Snoqualamie Pass? Their car ended up on its roof and the bottom of it just blended in with all the trees and rocks around them. They died of thirst, starvation, and exposure because nobody could find them."

"They were at the bottom of a ravine, Tommy. They probably died on impact."

He shook his head. "Why take the chance? Neon orange, baby. They'll be able to spot me at midnight."

I took another sip of my drink and raised my eyebrows. I'd heard of crazier things.

"So how 'bout you?" Tommy asked. "Rough day or are you here to play a game or two? Where's your board?"

The Hideout was a cop bar and in the past, after unusually difficult days I'd find myself there, unwinding with other police officers. Tommy and I had met at the Hideout when I was still on the force and he was hanging out with his brothers. We started playing chess and had played every week since. He was the one reason I still hung out there. "I found a friend of mine last night," I said. "We were going to have a drink together, but he was dead when I found him."

"The chess guy from the paper?"

I nodded. "That's him."

"He was the chess whiz friend of yours you told me about, right?" I nodded again. "What happened?" he asked.

"Looks like suicide," I said, "but I don't know."

Tommy shook his head and took a gulp of his drink. "I'm sorry to hear that, Ray. Losing a friend isn't easy. What about it don't you know?"

"It just doesn't feel right." I pushed my drink to the middle of the table and sat back.

Tommy nodded, drained his glass, and levered himself like a jack knife into a standing position. "I'll keep my ears open," he said. "Let me know if I might be of service."

"Thanks," I said. Having an informant in a cop bar could bring invaluable information. Tommy patted my shoulder like an old man might and trundled out of the bar, stopping to give the waitress a tip and a light slap on her rear. She then came over to collect Tommy's empty glass. I ordered a submarine sandwich and then checked my messages.

Cell phones were a wonderful invention. Mine was so small it could be a key chain tchotchke, but it let me send and receive e-mail, voice mail messages, play video games, take a picture—heck, I could even talk to someone if I had to.

There were two messages, both from John Keller. To paraphrase: If I didn't get my ass down to the precinct as soon as I could…blah, blah, blah.

His second message was equally eloquent: When I was told to make myself available, it didn't mean by message service! Blah, blah, blah.

I didn't care for that kind of commanding. When I was in high school, the track coach was a stick shaped man of fifty or sixty some odd years and wore shiny rayon sweat outfits with the pant legs tucked into his socks. He sat on a high director's chair like you saw on Hollywood movie sets, and from that seat—he was never on the track itself—Coach Tucker would bark commands from some magazine or book through an old cheerleader style bullhorn while he surreptitiously puffed cigarettes. He was a man without any running experience and we all knew it. In fact, one of my teammates had to teach me how to breathe properly during long distance running. There wasn't much to it, regular breaths, in through the nose and out the mouth. The idea was to keep oxygen to the working muscles. Pretty simple really, yet the guy barking orders never mentioned it. And, for what it's worth, Coach Tucker, after a chronic coughing fit, left in the middle of the third track meet of the season. He died of lung cancer a few months later.

I erased Keller's messages from my phone and ordered a slice of chocolate cake. I thought he could have been nicer since we hadn't seen each other in so long. I'd never responded well to barked orders.

5

☐ As with any sport or game, chess demands dedication and effort to master its fundamentals. To go beyond the basics takes study and practice—some talent doesn't hurt either. One advantage chess has over other games is the ability for a player or student to study the masters. The most brilliant performances by athletes of long ago are nothing more than myth because neither film nor videotape had been invented. Even with the variety of recording media available with modern technology, a basketball game can only be watched and mimicked. Chess, on the other hand, can be recorded move-by-move, then played again, move-by-move, allowing the person to study and learn—move-by-move, from all the past masters in the world while the game progressed.

When I'd found Charlie in the hotel room it was apparent to me, even if it wasn't to the police, that he'd been playing chess with someone. If Detective Keller had questioned the other players in the tournament, they may have given him the impression Charlie was probably just analyzing positions, just as Vladimir Penski had been doing when I talked to him. What Detective Keller would have failed to tell them was there were captured pieces on both sides of the board.

If two right-handed people played chess, the captured pieces were removed and tended to be placed naturally to the person's right, leaving pieces on both sides of the board. When a right-handed person played a lefty, the captured pieces ended up on the same side, but in two distinct camps. Finally, when one person played through a game, captured pieces, both black and white, ended up mingled together on one side.

The chessboard set up in Charlie's room had two groups of captured pieces on opposite sides of the board. After thinking about it, I decided I remembered Charlie as a right-hander, and I found his body on the side of the table where he would have been playing the white pieces. Ergo, two right-handed players.

I wanted to mess with Keller, so I ignored his orders and went home instead of to the police station. I recalled the picture I'd taken of the chessboard in Charlie's room from my cell phone and set up the same position with my own pieces and chessboard. I knew that to improve my game I needed to study the masters, but this time I hoped to find something beyond how to play a better game of chess.

BLACK

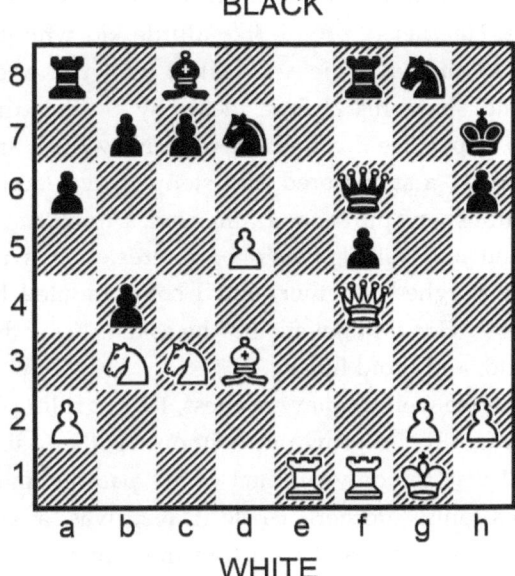

WHITE

Was Charlie behind the black pieces? I had my doubts simply because a shot to the head like the one he had taken wouldn't allow the victim to walk around for a more comfortable spot to sit down and die.

He had to have been playing the white pieces, but the most glaring oddity was the overturned king. In chess, laying down the king means resignation. The player only resigns when he has no hope of winning and calls it quits. But white had plenty of play in the position left on the board in Charlie's room. Besides, Charlie's motto had been, "No one wins by resigning." In fact, he'd written a book about chess strategy and tactics with that phrase as the title. It was published when he was twenty-six and on a meteoric rise within the chess community. He'd beaten all of the big names and won most of the major tournaments around the world, or at least finished in the top three. He was so proud, like a little kid who just lost his first tooth, when he was asked to write about his games and share his chessic ideals by putting them all down on paper. He'd called me from New York and told me in a rush, a stammered and stepped over account of how a publisher approached him after a tournament win in England and asked if he'd be interested in writing a book. We laughed together, and I congratulated him on his success. "Can you believe it?" he asked. Yes, I thought. Yes I could, and I told him so.

When we weren't playing chess, I was grilling Charlie about his family. I'd grown up without brothers, sisters or cousins. I was the only product of my parents' marriage; my dad's only brother, Uncle Dave, was a certified bachelor, and from what he'd told me, my mother's two twin sisters had estranged themselves from their family over a disagreement concerning the political and religious values of not only their parents, but of the President of the United States. Uncle Dave only knew my mother's version of the story of course, but from what he'd heard, at the age of nineteen, my aunts packed up what belongings they had, changed their names, and moved to a hippie commune somewhere in southern Oregon and were never heard from again. In fact, they probably had no idea I had been born. I knew my grandparents for a short time, but they all died before I reached the age of nine. Again, according to Uncle Dave, they were all heavy smokers and two of them succumbed to lung cancer while a heart attack and a stroke claimed the others.

Charlie Roggenbuck, on the other hand, came from a big family with ties all over the country. Charlie was the third of four brothers. The two older ones, Roger and Mathew, both joined the military right out of high school and went on to life-long careers in the Army. The younger brother, Alan, was an automotive whiz and eventually moved somewhere in the south where he was the lead mechanic for a popular NASCAR driver. Charlie also had a sister, Wendy, who was about five years younger than him. She joined the Peace Corps as soon as she'd earned a degree in sociology and was somewhere in Peru.

The Roggenbuck family hailed from rural Maryland, and it was no surprise to Charlie's parents when all of the kids packed up and left as soon as they could. It wasn't because life was bad; none of the kids were abused, neither mom nor pop were alcoholics, and there were no legal troubles following them around. The fact was that with such a large family, vacations to far away destinations were difficult to finance. Charlie's father, Seth, managed a grocery store and his mom, Barbara, was an accountant at a small radio station. They made enough to make the house payments and put food on the table and that was about it. However, everyone in the family was an avid reader, and when it came time to explore the world without the aid of books, each one of the kids did it in different ways. Charlie saved his money and found his way to the University of Washington on the opposite side of the country.

I pulled my copy of *No One Wins by Resigning* from the shelf and skimmed through the introduction until I found what I was looking for: Among all of the professional chess players ever recorded, Charlie Roggenbuck had the fewest resignations during major tournaments. He was a fighter and played until all hope was lost and it would be pointless to play any further.

A nice quick route to a solution in Charlie's case would have been for the police to find a solid fingerprint from one of the chess pieces in his hotel room and match it with someone at the tournament. Of course they weren't even looking because his death had been ruled a suicide.

When I finally called John Keller at the precinct, my apparent lack of cooperation with the Seattle Police Department had earned me a bad mark. "Get down here now or I'll have you arrested," Keller said.

"On what grounds?" I asked.

"Obstruction."

"You know you can't…" The connection clicked off, and I suddenly missed the days when I could slam the phone down on its cradle.

The West Seattle Police Precinct headquarters was on the corner of 8th and Virginia. Their territory covered everything from Seattle Center to Pioneer Square, which meant tourists, businesses and mobs of fans after Seahawks and Mariners games. The fluctuating myriad of people and crowds meant headaches to the cops, but that variety added spice to the job.

The West Seattle Precinct was also where my short ride with the Seattle P.D. played out and I was nervous going back there even though I'd left the police force voluntarily, before things got ugly and I would have been forced out.

My partner and I had been patrolling Pioneer Square, a popular historic and touristy area that had experienced a rash of armed robberies. Two restaurants and a gift shop had been hit by a guy wearing jeans, a sweatshirt jacket and a ski mask. Unfortunately, his description fit every down-on-his-luck Joe who wandered the area begging for bus fare. After the thief robbed a couple at gunpoint following a baseball game, though, the ski mask had shifted enough for them to notice a star-shaped tattoo on his neck.

Six days after that couple had lost their credit cards while looking down the barrel of a .45, my partner and I saw a tattoo shaped like a star gracing the neck of a young man in tattered blue jeans and looking like he belonged on a WANTED poster. The bulging outline of a semi-automatic pistol stuffed into the back of his pants didn't hurt my suspicion. We followed him into the Elliot Bay Book store on South Main Street and while he was perusing the current issue of *Playboy*, I stepped behind him and said, "Why haven't you used the credit cards yet?"

Star-neck was out the door before the centerfold landed face up on the floor. When I hit the street, I had a clear shot and I took it. I aimed low, but he tripped and took the round just below his shoulder.

Bad timing.

For both of us.

And things got worse from there.

6

I still had the phone in my hand, wondering if I should call Keller back and tell him where to go when the doorbell rang. It was three o'clock, which meant it was Kortnie Philips, the young woman I'd hired to walk my dog, Morphy, three times a week. "Hi, Kortnie," I said as I opened the door.

"Hey, Ray," she beamed, bouncing up on her toes. Kortnie was twenty-two and working on her degree in veterinary science. Her normally flowing hair was the color of dawn at the height of summer, but at the moment was stuffed under a bright red wool hat. During the warmer months she teased the boys by wearing tank tops and cut-offs, but in January, it was denim jeans and a bulky coat heavy enough to take on Mt. Rainier. I'd thought about taking advantage of the crush she had on me, but Kortnie was tortured by dramatics and often made Morphy wait—to his credit, patiently—while she tearily described her awful boyfriend, traitorous friends or unfair professors. While her body and mind were definitely adult, I wondered if her emotions had made it past eighth grade.

I let her in and closed the door. "How're you doing today?" I asked. She was still smiling which was a good sign.

"Okay. Well, you know." The smile dissolved into a sigh.

"Uh oh. Sounds like trouble in paradise." Kortnie belonged to the bizarre species of woman who never wanted the men who wanted her, choosing instead the guy who used her up and then made her feel the hurtful end of the relationship was her fault. And she believed it, too. "But I love him!" she'd say. She'd been through six loving and meaningful boyfriends in the two years I'd known her.

Kortnie nodded her head and looked up at the ceiling. She blinked quickly to stem the flow of tears.

Mentally I rolled my eyes and sighed, but Morphy saved me. He walked in wagging his tail and smiling as only a dog can. He instantly reversed Kortnie's mood. Morphy was my best buddy and was about as good a watchdog as my sofa, but I couldn't throw a Frisbee to an alarm system. Suddenly Kortnie's problems were forgotten—for the moment—and she was kneeling on the floor petting Morphy and rubbing his neck.

Man, I loved that dog.

"Kortnie," I said, "I'm sorry, but I really need to go. You going to be okay?"

She smiled at me. "Oh, sure. I'll lock up."

It was ridiculous to be nervous going into my old precinct. I'd left with my head held high. Leaving the force hadn't been easy, but it had been my decision, no one else's.

When I told the desk cop my name and asked to see John Keller, his eyes widened slightly and he nodded his head. Did he know who I was, or was he just shocked someone was there to see Keller?

"What took you so long?" John asked, coming around a glass partition.

"Traffic," I said.

"Ray, I know you weren't stuck on I-5 all day."

"Are these the questions you wanted me to come down here to answer, Detective?" I asked. "I'm sure the DOT would be more of an expert about the traffic in our city. Don't you?" His neck turned pink and he glanced at the Sergeant behind the desk who looked back innocently.

"Why don't you come back to my desk? The questions I have concern a case I'm working on," he said.

I smiled to myself. Detective John Keller was worried about being watched. Served him right.

John's lanky partner, Mark Peters, joined us at the desk and folded himself into a sitting position so he looked like a half open lawn chair. "Okay gentlemen," I said, "I'm here. What can I do for you?"

John drew a pen like a wand from his desk drawer and placed it with precision on a blank legal pad. "Detective Peters and I have been told you think your friend's suicide isn't what it appears to be."

"Oh? Who says that?" I asked.

"A couple of your chess buddies called us and said so. Is that true?"

"Yeah, I suppose it is. Are you going to open an investigation?"

John shook his head. "Not unless it's warranted. We don't normally investigate suicides, Ray. You know that. Seems to be a waste of taxpayer money when we try to figure out the obvious."

"So what am I doing here?"

"We need to know if you have any evidence. You brought up the question so you must have a reason to think Roggenbuck was murdered. So let's hear it."

"You made me come down here for that? You couldn't just ask over the phone?"

Keller looked at the surface of his desk to hide his smile. *Asshole*, I thought. "Fine," I said. "The game on the table where you found Charlie. He'd been playing someone."

"And?" Keller said. "He could have been playing that game the day before or earlier in the day."

"His body was right next to the table, John. He was sitting there when he died."

"Maybe he couldn't handle it any more. Maybe he was going to lose and offed himself instead."

"I hope that's not a professional observation, *Detective*," I said, "and I use that word loosely." I wouldn't say I disliked John Keller; it was more like I didn't respect him, the way Bugs Bunny didn't respect Elmer Fudd. It didn't help that John didn't seem to be taking Charlie's death seriously either.

"Careful, Ray," he said and his face solidified like a plaster cast.

"Just tell him, John," Peters said with a sigh. It was the first time I'd heard him speak since the hotel.

Keller shot a look at him then sat back in his chair. He tossed the pen on the desk and said, "Fine. The preliminaries are showing there was no gunpowder residue on the victim's hand. If he'd been holding the gun when the shot was fired, his hand would be covered with it."

"What? You knew this? When? Why am I here answering ridiculous questions when you already know he was murdered?"

"We needed to hear your theory. See if it adds up, if it contributes to our investigation." He stopped and glanced at his partner.

"What?" I said. "What else?"

Peters leaned forward in his chair and said, "We're not sure your idea of him playing someone will fly either. We didn't find any other fingerprints."

"Even on the chess pieces?" I asked.

"We found some partials," John said, "but nothing solid."

"Doesn't that seem strange?" I asked. "If Charlie was alone and analyzing, his prints should be on all the pieces."

"Well, I guess that would depend on how he held them."

I rolled my eyes, puffed up my cheeks, and blew air out. *Wow*, I thought. "Do you have any other questions for me, Detective?"

"Just one. Where were you between five and eight p.m. the day Roggenbuck was killed?"

"Are you kidding me, John?" I said. "You're accusing me now? Do you know what an investigation is? Accusing everyone in the immediate vicinity is what they do on TV! It doesn't really work!"

"You know damned well you're a viable suspect. A very large percentage of the murderers call 9-1-1 themselves as you know. The odds say you're a suspect."

"Dammit, just do your job! Do some real police work for a change, and get out there and find out who murdered my friend!" I stood quickly and knocked over the chair. The raised voices and the crash of overturned furniture turned heads our way.

"No need to get upset, Ray," John said quietly.

I set the chair upright and put on my coat with my back facing John Keller. "Nice talking to you Detective Peters," I said and left the station.

7

☐ I had been a good cop, but I couldn't deal with having killed someone by shooting him in the back and then having the whole thing dragged through the newspapers and evening newscasts as cheap entertainment. I left the force soon after the investigation was complete, even though I was found innocent of manslaughter. The bigger concern was that the investigation had blossomed from my partner's report of the incident. According to him, I had never identified myself as a police officer; nor had I warned the suspect before firing the fatal shot. We got our man, but the tactics were questionable. I'd replayed the scene, the entire day, over and over in my head but I just couldn't remember if I ID'd myself or not. I did know I didn't want to kill the guy. What I didn't know was if my partner, John Keller, smiled while writing his report, though I *was* sure he enjoyed every minute of my ordeal.

For the same reason, John and I had never clicked. We had nothing more than an impersonal professional relationship, more like doctor and patient than partners. I'd seen plenty of TV cops who were best friends with their partners and that seemed nice. I knew it was just television, but I also knew real cops like that, cops who ate dinner and went to ball games with their partners and their families.

It wasn't a friend I was in need of, but someone I knew I could trust, someone I didn't need to ask what his next move was because I would already know. What I got was a cold partner who I had to look sideways at.

John Keller was a by-the-book kind of guy. His uniform had been pressed with razor thin seams every day, and he walked so stiffly and straight I joked about him having a stick shoved so far up his ass it pushed his shoulders up. He didn't find it funny. I was nothing more than the person he got stuck working with. The problem was he didn't like being forced to team up with me; he would much rather have had Joe Friday.

The pudgy, wrinkled John Keller I'd been being harassed by now was a different story. What had happened to him since I'd left the force? What happened to the pressed clothes and spit-shined shoes? My guess was he was hell on partners and often got a talking to from his captain about laying off on the quoting of rules and regulations. Just a guess, but it seemed right. I didn't see a wedding band either. No doubt she got tired of his fastidiousness, too. Again, it was just a guess.

When I left Detectives Keller and Peters, my breath was shaky and my heart beat faster. Keller didn't have a clue in the Charlie Roggenbuck case, and Peters's head was in the clouds to the point he couldn't bother keeping track of earthbound conversations. That wasn't fair. Peters seemed okay. He probably just kept quiet most of the time to keep things peaceful between him and Keller.

No matter what Keller thought, Charlie had been playing someone. My experience as a chess player told me so, and my instinct as a cop backed it up.

As I drove up Virginia Avenue away from the police station, something Keller had said kept eating at me. They'd found partial fingerprints on the pieces. If somebody took the time to wipe the pieces clean of evidence, why bother putting them back on the chessboard? Was the murder planned? Every TV cop show talked about fingerprints so only the densest of criminals didn't do something to hide theirs. They wore gloves or used a towel to wipe down everything they touched. Either Charlie's murder was planned and his killer held the pieces daintily, only a portion of his fingertips moving the pieces like a Victorian lady drinking tea, or the pieces were wiped down and then replaced on the board. But why?

I pulled to the curb in front of the Youth Center. It was a converted warehouse between Elliot Avenue and Elliot Bay where kids who have nowhere else to go hang out. There were other places but pier side was popular because there was so much to do. Tourists were easy targets for panhandling, but there were also fast food restaurants for a cheap meal and odd jobs for pocket change. When the kids were bored with staying alive, there were plenty of things to watch out on the bay. The big cruise ships docked there along with the fast hydrofoils that zipped passengers through Puget Sound and dropped them off in Victoria, B.C.; military ships and big tankers eased past while gulls and pigeons careened overhead. If they had money, some of the kids blew it at the arcade or took in a movie, but the smart ones kept it pocketed with their next meal in mind.

I wanted to see how Alex was doing after hearing of Charlie's death, and I thought a game of chess would relax us both—or just me. I hadn't told him I thought foul play was suspected, but I was sure he'd heard something on the street or read the paper. Apparent suicides of famous people were rarely accepted as fact so quickly.

Inside, Mary Connors directed me to the game room where Alex was playing blitz against another boy. Their hands flew over the chessboard rattling the pieces and slapping the clock. Each boy stood over the board like a general managing his battle plans.

When the game was over, Alex was the one smiling. Both boys glanced around the room. When I was spotted, they gave one another a slight nod and I heard Alex say, "Later" to his opponent who then made for the opposite door. My guess was they had bet on the game of speed chess—which was against Youth Center rules—and checked before exchanging payment. I wasn't a counselor but I *was* an adult. Just as bad.

"Hey, Gordo," Alex said.

"How are you doing?" I asked. He shrugged and sat down behind the chessboard.

"So you found The Buck, huh?" he said.

"I told you I did," I said.

"No," he said, shaking his head. "You said when you got there he was dead. You didn't say you discovered the body."

I sat down across the board from him. "Yeah. I found him."

"Cops say he killed himself. Is that true?"

"Where did you hear that?" I asked. I didn't think kids read newspapers anymore.

"Around."

"Well I don't think so," I said.

"So someone killed him."

Alex said it as a statement, and I nodded, not knowing how much he'd ask or how much I was willing to discuss. "Why?" he said after a minute. "He was the best! He was going to win the Championship. You said so yourself."

I nodded again. Before the tournament Alex and I had played over many of Charlie's games, though at that point I'd never told him I'd been friends with "The Buck." In my heart and in my gut, I felt a chess player had killed Charlie but I didn't want to ruin Alex's image of America's top talents. "People do stupid things for stupid reasons, Alex. Maybe somebody killed him because he was the best. Or maybe he cut someone off in traffic and they followed him back to the hotel. Who knows?"

8

☐ After a day off to regroup, the players in the US Chess Championships resumed their games. I found Nigel Cross, the organizer of the event, in the Northwest building of the Seattle Center, standing near the middle of the Rainier Room where the tournament was being held.

Nigel's parents were British nationals, but he had been born in New York while they were interviewing for professorships at NYU. He grew up with a watered-down accent and a remarkably jumbled view of American history—particularly "that confounded disagreement over tea" known as the Revolutionary War.

To no one's surprise, Nigel majored in mathematics instead of history.

Chess was something of a hobby for him at first. Nothing more than a diversionary game with his friends until they talked him into entering a local school tournament. After he won the tournament hands down, chess became an extracurricular activity as well as a course of study. But the win turned out to have been a fluke. Nigel never won another tournament and, discouraged, he dropped out of tournament play. He never lost his love for the game though, and instead of playing in tournaments, Nigel Cross began organizing them and his true talent in the chess arena blossomed.

In the Rainier Room he stood against the middle of the far wall. His eyes scanned the playing tables and watched the arbiters as they moved throughout the room like watchdogs. He was about five-six and stout. His hair was wavy and graying; his steely eyes all seeing. When they locked on me crossing the room, they dimmed a little as he tried to remember who I was. We'd never actually met, though I'd played in two tournaments he'd put together.

"Mr. Cross," I whispered as I reached him. "I wonder if I might have a moment of your time?" The room was quiet, like a library, only the occasional scratch of pen on paper, thumps of chess pieces, or the hollow *chunk* of a clock's timer. A few people stood against the walls or looked in the doorway. They were hushed like spectators at the 18th hole of the Masters just before the underdog makes the winning putt.

Nigel Cross glanced at the arbiters and motioned me toward the hallway. "How can I help you?" he asked.

"My name is Ray Gordon. I'm looking into the death of Charlie Roggenbuck."

"What is there to look into?"

I shrugged. "Let's just say I'm unconvinced."

"You're a private investigator then?" he asked.

"I'm a former police officer working on my own. Charlie was a friend of mine."

"Is that so?" he said. "I didn't think Mr. Roggenbuck had any friends left."

"What do you mean by that?"

"If you're a friend, Mr. Gordon, you know perfectly well what I mean."

"We hadn't seen each other for a while, Mr. Cross, so I don't have any idea what you're talking about."

"I see. Well, Charlie changed a few years ago. He became very closed off from his colleagues and his behavior was, shall we say, erratic. He would be friendly and talkative one moment then sullen, angry, even depressed the next. There have been rumors of gambling debts, though those are just rumors. He used to be so jovial, but players began to stay away from him."

Since I hadn't seen Charlie in some time, any of his behavioral oddities could have been true. Physically he'd gained a few pounds but that could have easily been part of getting older. Charlie had always been able to eat a lot, and he never seemed to gain weight. There was a café near campus where we would often go late at night, usually for fries and coffee, sometimes for dinner. When he was really hungry, he would order the largest meal they had, ask them to double it and throw in a slice of pie. It became known as "Charlie's Special" and actually became a menu item until they went out of business. It was three times as much food as anyone else ate, but he never showed any ill effects. "Crazy metabolism," he would say.

I shook my head. "I'm sorry, Mr. Cross. What was that?"

"I said his adherence to our Code of Ethics was questionable."

"Questionable?"

"It was rumored he may have had outside help during a few tournaments." Outside help could mean anything from flagrant cheating by using some sort of electronic means to receive moves to collaborating with players to throw the match.

"Including this one?" I asked.

"I'm sure we'll never know now. Anybody who may have been involved with him in that regard has nothing to gain by admitting it."

The very idea of Charlie cheating was shocking to me. Charlie was in love with chess. I'd seen people treat their spouses with less affection than Charlie caressing a finely carved chess piece. "Mr. Cross, why is the Championship continuing? Shouldn't it be cancelled and reorganized since one of the players is dead?"

Cross nodded his head and glanced at his watch. "We were planning to cancel it actually. But after discussing it with the police, we decided it was still early enough to adjust the rounds."

"What did the police have to do with it?"

"I'm not sure I'm at liberty to say."

"I'm an ex-cop, Mr. Cross, and Detective Keller is my old partner. It's okay."

He nodded while he looked into the playing room. "Detective Keller seems to think the person behind Mr. Roggenbuck's death is one of our chess players."

"When did he tell you that?" I asked.

"Actually, not too long before you arrived."

9

☐ My place was a small three bedroom, one and a half bath with redwood siding. It sat on a nice patch of grass near Magnolia overlooking Puget Sound and the Olympic Mountains to the west, downtown Seattle and the Cascade Mountains to the east. On windy days, three old Douglas firs in my front yard swayed back and forth like drunks huddled around a trash can fire. For the past six years, I'd shared the house with Morphy. He'd been the Humane Society's mutt of the week on the local news and since I was a sucker for puppy dog eyes, I paid an extra hundred bucks to make sure he came home with me. He was part Labrador retriever and part Greyhound so he had a sleekness to go with his lovable goofy face. His coat was the color of wheat just before harvest time with a thin stripe of white between his eyes and over his nose like a paintbrush stroke. Morphy was the only family I had and he never left the toilet seat down. He had his own door leading out to our fenced-in backyard and was spoiled by

Kortnie, who gave him treats during their walks. I did the same whenever I could.

When I got home from the Seattle Center, it was raining and the wind pushed angrily at the trees, which suited my mood just fine. John Keller had only what I'd told him. He'd wanted me at the station, not as a witness, but as a cop because he needed something, anything, to show the captain. He'd been counting on Charlie's death being a suicide, but with no gunpowder residue on the victim's hands, he didn't have any place to start his investigation. I shook my head and kicked a ragged tennis ball across the floor. Morphy wagged his tail and licked the back of my hand. I grunted and walked by him. Poor dog.

I put in a Wynton Marsalis CD and sat down at my chess table. A former adult student and friend who had been the Rembrandt of woodworking had given me an extraordinary handmade chessboard and I kept it and a set of pieces on the table, always ready for a game or some analysis.

The position from Charlie's last game was still set up. I picked up the White King and examined it for the umpteenth time since I'd bought the set years ago. It was heavy on my palm, formidable for a game piece. The wood was the color of ancient bone, but warmer, with dark shades of grain undulating across the surface like the lines of a contour map. Smooth to the touch, it was perfectly turned from the wide base, gracefully tapering in the middle to join the crown and topped with a delicately carved cross to signify his majesty. To keep from scratching the board, the underside of the base was covered with bright green billiard cloth.

Chess was so much more than a game. It was art. The beginning position of a chess match was formed by two identical armies of contrasting colors facing one another from opposite sides of the board. The beauty was apparent in the symmetry of the pieces; the art was in the tension. Once the game began, the equality was broken, the pieces created different patterns on the board, and both the beauty and art of chess were found in the myriad possibilities of the position.

I placed the King back on the board and listened to the mellow tones of a trumpet resonate through the room. I wiped away all thoughts of John Keller and his impotent policing skills and then sank into the game before me.

BLACK

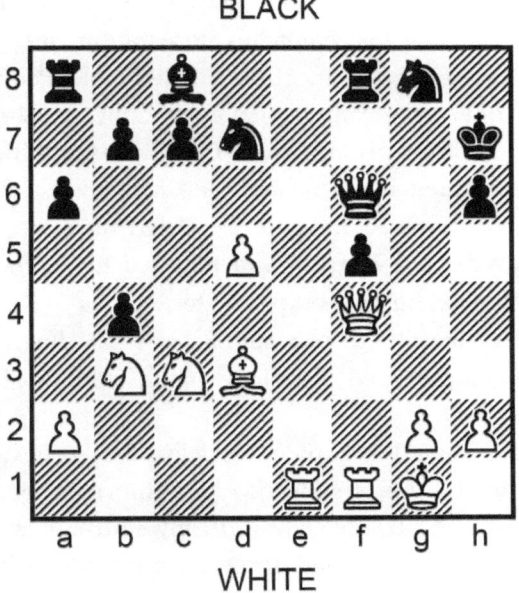

WHITE

Assuming the rules of chess had been followed, Charlie resigned on his turn—if he had indeed resigned. Looking at the position of the pieces though, I saw no reason for him to have given in. Rook to e6, for example, sacrificed the Knight at c3 but lured the Queen away from her King and gave White an excellent attack.

I stared at the multitudes of variations Charlie might have played in the game and the room around me faded away as the sun sank below a bank of clouds pushing against the Olympic Mountains. At last Morphy whimpered to remind me neither of us had had any dinner.

In the kitchen, I dished out a couple scoops of kibble for Morphy and made myself a peanut butter and jelly sandwich—extra jelly—and poured a glass of milk. Morphy sat on his haunches looking at me with a bemused stare while I ate at the kitchen table. People who didn't know dogs might have thought he was well mannered, letting his master eat first. It was nothing of the sort. He wanted my sandwich *and* his bowl of crunchy brown liver-flavored nuggets. I resisted his stare, and he finally gave a bored grunt and plodded to his food dish when I showed him my empty plate.

After catering to our stomachs, I sat down at my computer and typed Charlie's name into an Internet search engine.

There were biographies, articles, and a few stories related to his recent death. Nothing mentioned the possibility of Charlie cheating during tournament games as Nigel Cross had alleged. If there were any suspicions of a Grandmaster eliciting outside help during a game, the Internet should have been jammed with speculations, rumors, and theories. So was Cross lying or was the suspicion held by only a select few? If he was lying, why?

I surfed the Internet to the US Chess Championship homepage. It had biographies of all the players but nothing that linked any of them together in a scandal. There were dozens of national and international chess events, so it was a given they all had played one another at some point or other during their careers. What I was looking for was gossip, rumor, or flat out proof of Charlie and another chess player cheating or having some sort of public dispute suggesting a potential motive for murder. I found nothing.

After graduating from the University of Washington, Charlie had gone back to New York to get into the restaurant business with his cousin. He'd told me at the time that he had no real interest in being a cook, a waiter, or anything else associated with his cousin's restaurant, but it was a job in New York. That was the key. Chess players from all over the world came to New York, lived there, played there, studied, and taught there. To Charlie, New York was chess. If he was going to make a name for himself in the chess community, it would be in New York. As far as I knew, he wasn't involved with the restaurant anymore, it had been years since we'd graduated from the University of Washington, but it was a good place to start. Too bad I didn't know either the name of the restaurant or the cousin. On a whim, I typed in the name Roggenbuck and instructed the Internet to search under New York restaurants. There were plenty of results about Charlie, but none of them were about the restaurant. At least not within the first twenty pages I waded through.

I turned off the computer and called Carla. I doubted if she'd remember the name of Charlie's cousin, but maybe talking about it would help jar something loose in my brain. "Hey are you busy?" I asked when she answered.

"Not too busy," she said airily. "What's up?"

"You wouldn't happen to remember the name of the cousin Charlie went back to New York to work for do you?"

"Uh, not off the top of my head. Why? What's going on, Ray?"

I told her about Keller calling me down to the police station and how he'd opened a murder investigation. "I don't think he really has much to go on except for the fact that they know he wasn't holding the gun when it was fired. They'll start asking questions now, though."

"I'm not sure if that's good news or bad," Carla said.

"I know what you mean, but at least we know Charlie didn't kill himself."

"Why are you trying to find his cousin?"

"Because from what I hear Charlie changed a bit over the last few years. Apparently, he wasn't his jolly old self and there are all kinds of rumors about gambling and cheating. I thought talking to his cousin about it was a good first step."

"Tony," Carla said.

"What?"

"The cousin's name was Tony. I don't know his last name though."

"Are you sure?" I asked.

"Yep. Remember that night we all piled into his car?"

I thought back to our college days. "Uh…" I said.

Carla giggled. "You know, that night he got burned?"

Then I got it. It was our third year, and Carla wanted to see a movie that had just come out. She asked me to go with her, I asked Charlie if he wanted to go and he asked Rich Newburg, a chemistry major from Spokane we'd all met at the music recital of one of Carla's girlfriends. Rich asked if he could bring a couple of girls he knew which was fine since one of them had caught Charlie's eye a week before. There were six people going to the movie and we had one car, a bright yellow 1974 Volkswagen Bug owned by one Charlie Roggenbuck. He asked me to drive because he wanted to sit in back with Rich and the girls would sit on their laps.

We piled in, everyone laughing and joking, had just left campus and were headed for the movie theatres when Charlie started screaming, "Stop the car! Stop the car!" I didn't stop but Carla twisted around to see what was going on. Charlie started to squirm and the girl on his lap looked like she was riding a bull in a tiny enclosed rodeo.

"Seriously, Gordon," Charlie yelled. "Stop the car, my ass is on fire!"

I pulled to a stop and Charlie wrestled his way out from the back seat. He hopped up and down on the sidewalk and rubbed his palm over his backside as people stared. "What happened?" Carla asked.

Charlie stopped bouncing long enough for us to see a patch of reddened skin through a quarter-sized hole burned through his jeans. "What the hell?" Rich said.

I ducked back into the car and saw a similar sized hole melted through the vinyl that covered the seat where Charlie had been sitting. He poked his head in the other side, and we lifted the seat up to discover the culprit.

In a testament to German efficiency, the battery in a Volkswagen Bug was placed under the backseat. It made access to it easy and kept it out of the small engine compartment. The stuffing under the backseat was mostly gone and the extra weight of the girls forced the springs of the seat down on the battery terminals, made a connection and heated up. Charlie was only partially right about his ass being on fire. Technically, his ass had been electrocuted.

I laughed and said, "How could I forget that? But what's that got to do with the cousin?"

"Charlie was bragging about going to New York after he graduated, remember? He thought that would impress that girl who was sitting on him."

I nodded to myself. "That's right. He used a New York accent and called him 'Ant-nee' instead of Anthony. Ant-nee…"

"Druga!" Carla and I said together.

"Tony Druga," I said. "New York restaurateur. Thanks, Carla. I knew I could trust your memory."

"You got it, bub. Oh, by the way, my mom needs your help again."

"What happened?" Ever since I'd met Carla's mom she had been asking me to help her with small repair jobs, household chores, and light maintenance issues. I teased Carla about her mom having a crush on me, but it was really about Mrs. Caplicki trying to make me see my relationship with her daughter clearer.

"She did something to her vacuum cleaner. I'm sure nothing too dramatic though," Carla said

"Okay. I'll get over there tomorrow."

"Thanks. Let me know if I can help you with anything else."

I disconnected with Carla and called information. Then I dialed the number for Tony Druga in New York, but it was Tony's wife, Andrea, who answered the phone. Anthony, "and you better not call him that, he goes by Tony," she said, was on his way to Seattle to pick up Charlie's body and take care of his affairs.

"What affairs?" I asked. "I thought when Charlie graduated from UW, he and everything he had went to New York."

"Oh no," she said. "Charlie's girlfriend was in Seattle. It's so sad, what happened to them."

"What happened?" I asked.

"You don't know?"

I shook my head like I was standing in front of her then said, "No, I never heard."

"Well," she started, then there was a rustling noise, and I imagined she was maneuvering into a more comfortable position for full-on gossip mode, "they met when Charlie came home after college. At a chess tournament of all places, but for him it must have been heaven. You know, meeting a girl interested in chess and all. Anyway, they had a kind of on again, off again relationship because it was a long distance kind of thing, and he was always traveling to play chess."

"Long distance?" I said. "Where was she from?"

"Pennsylvania if I remember right," she said. "Anyway, her family was very strict, traditional, religious, you know, all that. So she wouldn't let him meet her parents. Well, she got pregnant and since they weren't married it was big trouble." Her voice went quiet and she whispered, "She was still living with them at the time."

"Was she underage?"

"Naw, just lived there I guess. Anyway, she was so scared of her father she broke up with him and moved out there to Seattle, but Charlie wanted to be with her and the baby. I swear I shoulda wrote it down and sent it to my favorite soap opera, ya know?" I nodded again, but didn't say anything. "But the sad part is Charlie was over in Europe at one of his chess tournaments when she had the baby. We heard it died after only a couple of hours, and she told Charlie she couldn't be with him because he reminded her of the baby and she just wanted to start over."

"Why did she come to Seattle?"

"I guess because she liked it when they went there together once. Maybe because it was as far away as she could get from her bastard of a father, I don't know. This all happened a few years ago, but when Charlie was there for this latest Championship he called and said he'd found her."

"Really? Do you know her name?" I asked.

"You know, I don't remember. For such a long time he wouldn't even talk about her or that period in his life. Besides, I'm so bad with names. I don't even remember yours to tell the truth! Wait a minute; I think it was something with an S sound…Sally, Cindy, Sandy. Something like that. Tony will know."

She gave me the number of Tony Druga's flight and said he was arriving that same night.

"Mrs. Druga," I said, "has anyone from the Seattle Police Department contacted you?"

"Nope. Just you."

"Thanks," I said. I shook my head when I hung up the phone. How could John Keller call himself a cop?

10

☐ Tony Druga looked like he could have been Charlie's brother. I'd been worried about spotting him coming off the plane, but there was no mistaking it. It was like seeing an old sepia-toned photograph of one of Charlie's ancestors from the early nineteen hundreds. I was amazed at how genes made family look alike. He was a big man, but not fat, with Popeye forearms and wiry black hair crawling out from under his shirt collar. I envisioned him in a greasy white cook's apron wielding heavy iron skillets like plastic spatulas.

Don't call him Anthony, I thought. Do not call him Anthony. "Anthony Druga?" I asked—*Damn!*—and stepped in front of him.

"Tony," he said. "Who are you?"

He smelled like burnt bacon. "My name's Ray Gordon. I was a friend of Charlie's." He let go of his suitcase and folded his arms. Those forearms were like trees. "Charlie and I met in college. The last time I saw him alive was a few years ago in Las Vegas."

"Yeah, okay. How do you know me?" he asked.

I explained how Charlie had mentioned his name in college and about the discussion I'd had with his wife. "I know the cop in charge of the investigation, and he doesn't have a clue," I said. "I want to find out who killed Charlie."

Tony nodded and I followed him through Sea-Tac airport. He wasn't much of a conversationalist and kept his lips as tight as the grip he had on his suitcase. I told him how Charlie and I had met through an ad for chess lessons and how we played chess during classes on small travel boards hidden behind stacks of books. After college, Charlie and I didn't see each other often, but we played in a lot of the same tournaments around the country and we always got together then. The last time I'd seen him was in Las Vegas a few years earlier and while I knew he was in Seattle for the US Championships, I hadn't expected him to call, but was glad when he did.

"Until I got to his room, of course," I said.

Tony Druga and I had walked the length of the airport and stood at the row of glass doors leading out to the taxi stand. He had said nothing to me within the last ten minutes and except for the occasional sideways glance from under his dark overgrown eyebrows, I never would have thought he knew I was there.

"Can I give you a ride into Seattle?" I asked.

"Sure. What the hell?"

We trekked across the vast acreage of pavement until we located my Land Cruiser. He tossed his suitcase into the back like a pillow and I asked, "How come you came to get Charlie?"

"What do you mean?"

I shrugged. "Why not one of his brothers or mom and dad?"

Tony smiled sadly. "My cousins are too far away. They'll be there for the funeral, but they couldn't come to Seattle first. Barb and Seth are too old. Just hearing about Charlie's death about killed them. They called and asked me to take care of it."

We strapped on our seatbelts and I eased out of the parking lot. "Your wife said Charlie had a baby that died," I said as we traveled north on I-5. "Do you know anything about it?"

In the passing lights, I saw his down turned mouth and bushy V-shaped eyebrows making his face a scrunched up X. "Everything was about chess to Charlie," he said. "He was supposed to be a partner with me, but instead he played chess. But that was okay, I knew he was good and was starting to become a big shot. I don't know a horse from a castle, but, you know, whatever." A shiver ran through me when he said 'horse' and 'castle'—were 'Knight' and 'Rook' really that difficult to remember? —but I shrugged and feigned agreement so he would continue. "It was good for a long time. He'd come in and help at the restaurant occasionally you know, but after he found out about the baby, he shut down. After that, his every waking moment was about chess. He quit helping at the restaurant, hardly spoke to anyone, and just played chess. We hardly talked to each other after that, and when we did we just argued, you know?" I nodded. He crossed his arms again and stared at the looming Seattle skyline.

"I don't remember him ever seeing anyone, let alone having a baby," I said. Tony remained silent. "Look, I know you don't know me from this side of Tuesday, but I can help."

"How can you help? My cousin is already dead."

"I want to find out who did it."

"Why do you care?"

"I found him, that's why. He was my friend, and I don't want the image of him lying on the floor to be my last memory of him, okay? I'm going to do this. Now, can you tell me who this woman is? Why didn't Charlie ever mention her?"

Druga stared at me for a beat and then said, "Charlie was never someone to talk about his personal life. He only talked about chess, sometimes about our restaurant." He kept his eyes forward as if he were seeing his cousin's life play out on the windshield. "I don't even know her last name; we never met because Charlie either never brought her to New York or she didn't want to come. It might have had something to do with her family. I don't know. But when he called last week, after he arrived for the US Championship, he said she was here."

"Was he upset about seeing her again? What's her name?" I asked.

"Her name is Sara. That's all I know, but no, he wasn't upset at all. He was definitely happy about it."

"Your wife told me you're here to take back the body and take care of Charlie's affairs." Tony nodded. "What affairs? What's here besides the mystery woman?"

Tony shook his head. "Nothing. I found her number in Charlie's phone book, and Andrea talked her into meeting with me. We want her to know how devastated

Charlie was when he found out the kid died and that we are still a family for her."

"That's nice of you. Where will you meet?" I asked.

"At her church," Tony said.

I thought that sounded very cloak and dagger but to each their own. "What church?" I asked. Tony's eyes narrowed and he faced me, arms still crossed. "Well, I might know where it is," I said quickly. "I know you don't know me, Tony, but I really do want to help. I'm not going to mug you. Geez, look at your arms compared to mine. I just want to get to the bottom of all this."

Tony's face had been like stone, but then he softened and quietly said, "Yeah. Okay."

I smiled. "So what church?"

He pulled a tightly folded piece of notebook paper from his jacket pocket and tipped it toward the window. "Saint Nicholas Russian Orthodox," he said, reading it in bursts as we passed streetlights.

"I know where it is," I said with a nod. "It's up on Capitol Hill. Looks like a miniature Kremlin with little turban-topped turrets. I can take you up there tomorrow if you want."

"I'll think about it," he said, his eyes again fixed forward. "Give me your number, and I might call you. Okay?"

"Okay."

Tony Druga had booked a room at the same place where his cousin had been murdered. I didn't ask if his choice of hotel was out of some sense of morbid curiosity, but chose instead to focus on the lovely woman who had smiled at me from behind the lobby counter. Tony thanked me and waved me off from the curb, probably not realizing I'd be at the Saint Nicholas Russian Orthodox Church whether I got a phone call from him or not.

11

☐ The Capitol Hill district in Seattle was where local political aficionados in the late eighteen hundreds lobbied for the foundation of state government to take root. That distinction, however, went to the city of Olympia and today Capitol Hill was known for its local color. It was filled with bars, clubs, and an eclectic mix of shops and galleries. Bronze footprints were embedded in the sidewalks outlining dance steps, and the mix of ethnic restaurants made Capitol Hill a favorite destination for people of all palates.

Seattle-ites liked Capitol Hill because it was generally tourist free. Most out-of-towners stuck to the fish-throwing extravaganza that was Pike Place Market while only true fans of martial-arts phenomenon Bruce Lee made their way through the hodge-podge of the district to Lake View Cemetery where he was buried.

There were several restaurants I frequented, but I wasn't familiar with the church's neighborhood, so I parked on 13th Avenue and crossed the street. St. Nicholas Russian Orthodox Church was a small yellow brick building with a group of slender spires, the soft blue tops of which bulged at the bottom and tapered to a point like Hershey's Kisses. I went inside and was greeted by every color in the spectrum as well as a few blends. I'd expected a somber, dim interior conducive to prayer and inner contemplation, but the walls were bright sky-blue and covered with paintings and murals of serious looking Russian saints, clergy and countrymen.

About a third of the way into the church, a wooden, beautifully carved partition with three big doors divided the building and rose about twenty feet without touching the arched ceiling. The center door was open and revealed an altar but I couldn't tell if anyone was there. The rails, lecterns and kneelers were rich wood and also carved with great detail. Colorful statues of saints and banners with biblical phrases filled the rest of the room.

There were no pews so I sat on a folding chair up in the small choir section at the back of the church and tried to look pious. The ringer on my cell phone was off, and I set it in the songbook pocket hanging off the back of the chair in front of me so I could see the screen in case Tony Druga should call—though I didn't expect him to. The look on his face the night before had said *thanks, but no thanks*. In case he spotted me, I'd brought along a rather dashing moustache to glue to my upper lip as a disguise, but I felt ridiculous for even considering it. If any cop I knew heard of me doing such a thing I would have to move out of state.

I unzipped the backpack I'd brought along and took out my travel chess set, the three-ring binder containing my games and the postcard I'd received before leaving for the church. More and more, my mailbox was being fed junk. Grocery store ads, credit card pleas and craftily phrased membership offers posing as tax-evasion alerts were all part of my daily trip to the garbage can. What made it worthwhile were the occasional postcards hidden like buried treasure within the daily stacks of paper slag. They didn't have shiny pictures of faraway places and none of them contained the words, "Wish you were here." Instead they were plain white 3x5 cards with archaic looking codes scribbled on the back. They were replies from people I was playing correspondence chess with, and the codes were notation, a way of writing down moves.

The postcard I'd brought was from Simon Waller, a professor from London, England. Our game was almost two years old, and we'd been writing small notes and getting to know one another. He taught ancient European history at the University of Greenwich and was an antiques buff. He was interested in my past as a police officer, short though it was, and had been giddy when I made him aware of my friendship with Charlie Roggenbuck whom he thought was going to be the next World Chess Champion too.

I kept all of my correspondence games in the binder, so I could keep a record of the moves along with all of the cards my opponents sent. It took only one disagreement about a mistaken move to prove to me that accurate record keeping was the key to a smooth correspondence chess game.

I found the game I was playing with Simon and set the pieces up on the board. I followed the score sheet in the binder and played through the game up to the last move I'd sent nearly a month before. Then I noted Simon's move from the postcard: *44. ...g4* and then moved the piece on the board.

BLACK

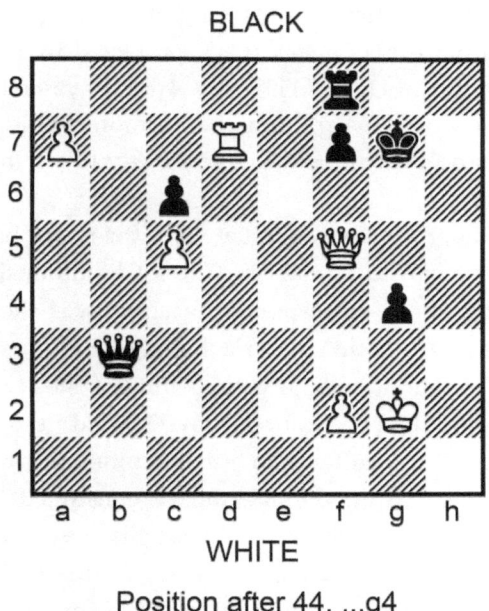

Position after 44. ...g4

Simon controlled the black pieces and moved his pawn forward a square to g4, so I wouldn't just nab it with my Queen and place his King in check.

We were forty-four moves into the game with an even amount of material. I really needed to be careful. As I scanned the board for possibilities, it looked like it would take a move to mobilize my rook and get it to a square where it could help in the attack on Simon's King. I also had the pawn on a7, which could be promoted to a Queen given the chance. If I could protect the a8 square with either my Queen or Rook, I could advance the pawn; promote it to a Queen and force Simon to capture it. Then I'd have a Queen and rook against his Queen.

But my King wasn't exactly safe either. If I couldn't significantly threaten Simon's King, it would give him the chance to place his Queen at h3, protected by his pawn, and place me in check. The only square available to my King then would be g1 and then Simon would look to bring his rook across to h8. Then I would be in serious trouble.

Luckily, the game wasn't an over the board battle like those being played at the US Chess Championship. The great thing about correspondence chess was the lack of time pressure. I didn't have a ticking clock next to the board as a reminder of my time limit. Instead, I had a calendar and enjoyed leisurely days to study the position and make a move rather than hurried minutes.

The position on the chessboard consumed me, and while I enjoyed the mental analysis the way a physicist might pore over the academic notes of Albert Einstein, I still felt lucky at not having to stay at the church too long. Tony Druga appeared within an hour. He took a folding chair and walked towards the front, near the ornate partition that opened up to reveal the altar, and sat down. He cleared his throat loudly, and while I put away my chess set, a man dressed in black walked out from somewhere behind the partition and shook Tony's hand. The clergyman was doughy and had a bushy, rust-colored beard surrounding his already round cheeks like a wreath.

They spoke briefly, the priest often raising his hands and speaking passionately but quietly. Tony finally shrugged, wrote something on a piece of paper which he then handed to the priest, and then left. He never looked about the place and Sara, Charlie's mystery woman, never made an appearance. My inner cop told me it looked like a drug deal. The deacon followed Tony with his eyes and then glanced at me with a nod and smile.

I took it as a sign.

"My name's Ray Gordon," I said after I went down to meet the deacon. "I have a very big favor to ask of you."

12

☐ I knew nothing about the practice of the Russian Orthodox faith but presumed anything I told the deacon would be confidential. So, after introducing myself and telling Deacon Kamalov everything about the case, I only asked that he tell Sara about me and that I wanted to solve a crime. That was it. I gave him my cell phone number and left the church.

At eleven seventeen I called the Westin Hotel and asked for Tony Druga. "Yo," he said when we were connected.

"Tony, this is Ray Gordon. Do you remember me?"

"Sure. Hey, sorry, but I already went to the church this morning," he said.

"Did you meet with Sara?" I asked conversationally.

"Nope. She didn't show."

"That's too bad," I said. "I was wondering if you'd care for some lunch? I'm buying."

"Mr. Gordon," he said, and then paused.

In my experience pauses meant an internal struggle about whether to tell a secret or not. "Tony?" I said, hoping to prompt him. "Anything you can think of might help me. No matter how trivial it might seem."

"Yeah, yeah. Okay. One month ago maybe, Charlie was looking for a man we know from New York. He was, you know, a mob guy."

"Charlie was looking for someone in the mob?" I asked, surprised.

"Well, not a mob guy *per se*. More like a street tough. He was a loan shark but he isn't in New York anymore. He's out here now. In Washington State."

"Tony, do you know this man's name? And where he is?"

"Name's Sam Scott. But I don't know where he's at. I think he runs a casino. That's all I know."

"Okay. Thank you, Tony. I think this will help me."

"Good. I talked to Andrea last night, and we appreciate what you're trying to do, you know? I'm outta here today, so we thought maybe you should know that."

"All right, Tony. Thank you. If you think of anything else, anything that may be of use, please call me anytime."

"Yeah, sure. Thanks for the ride from the airport."

"You're welcome." I smiled when I disconnected. Maybe I'd just caught a break.

Company or not, I was hungry and not really in the mood to cook. I went home again, grabbed my laptop, and then headed back down the hill to Red Mill Burgers on Dravus Avenue. Not only did they have the best hamburgers in town, they also let me use my laptop to play chess on the Internet while I ate.

Internet chess was as wonderful as it was dangerous. The great thing was the World Wide Web didn't stop at just providing information about the royal game. It let me log on to a chess-playing site and within seconds start a game with someone on the far side of the planet.

Most of the chess played on-line was blitz—the entire game was played in less than fifteen minutes; or lightning—the whole game in two to five minutes.

Anyone with a gambling problem would say it was the rush, not the money that provided the thrill. The Internet chess addict would claim the same thing but replaced the word money with time. I've spent hours, double digit hours, playing game after game on the Internet. Sometimes I got hooked up with a kid in Detroit sneaking a game during his computer class, sometimes a nurse in London on her break, a lawyer in Australia trying to wind down after a day in court, or a Grandmaster from Russia feeding on the inexperienced. You never knew who was playing.

To the credit of the waitresses at Red Mill Burgers, they only let me eat one hamburger and down a milkshake before they would good-naturedly kick me out.

I played six games of blitz chess during the course of my meal and then found a chat room where people were lobbing questions about opening moves, endgame study and the players at the US Chess Championship.

Some were furious the tournament was continuing after Charlie's death. Many had favored him as coming out on top of the pile. That was something Alex had mentioned when I'd first told him about Charlie's death: Was Charlie's murder prompted by fear? Fear of his skill? Was someone afraid of being unable to defeat him over the chessboard? Or were Charlie's alleged gambling problems involved somehow? A wager on the underdog would bring in a pretty sum if the favored player were out of the picture.

While I was on the police force, I'd helped in the arrest of a man who'd murdered his wife because she sneezed while a sports score was being given on TV, obliterating the announcer's voice. He shot her in the forehead without warning. We arrived after a neighbor reported the shot, and the husband didn't put up a fight, never said a word. He did ask us if we knew who'd won the game, though. We didn't tell him.

Who knew why someone blew out Charlie's skull? Fear? Ego? Money? Boredom?

I sent my own question into cyberspace: Who killed Charlie Roggenbuck and why?

Three people immediately confessed to the crime. Seven answers were excellent examples in the use of profanity, and someone else claimed it was proof Lee Harvey Oswald was alive. The rest were just as useless. So ended my session with modern communication technology.

13

☐ I drove over to Carla's mom's house and parked in the driveway. It was a two story white colonial with forest green trim and a yard suitable for a magazine cover. I got out of the car and ambled up to the house, wondering if the place had looked as good when Carla was growing up there.

Like me, Carla was an only child. Her mother, Rita, was a retired nurse while her dad, Randy, was a sales executive with a big computer company. Right after Carla graduated from high school, her parents divorced. Apparently, her dad had been seeing a young blond code developer for some time. When Rita found out about it, they decided to wait until Carla graduated before telling her. Carla already knew something was up though. She'd heard the fights and seen her dad sneaking phone calls. He was out of the house and living in Puyallup before Carla returned her cap and gown. She still received

Christmas and birthday cards from him, but that was the extent of her communication with her father.

I knocked on Mrs. Caplicki's door and waited. She didn't ask me to help with all of her home repair projects, just the smaller ones, but I certainly wasn't going to turn her down. Not too long ago, I'd been hurt, and she opened her home to me and let me stay long enough to recover. It was nice having Carla and her mom around, and it was about then that I finally realized what was missing in my life.

The door swung open, and Mrs. Caplicki stood beyond the threshold with a look on her face that made me wonder if I was late or not the person she was expecting. She was about five-nine with long dark hair and a statuesque body I knew she worked hard to keep fit. She was a die-hard yoga class attendee and went to the gym often enough to know the employees on a first name basis. She reminded me of the glamorous women film stars of the nineteen forties who always looked ready for a drive, a picnic, or a night on the town. Her hair was never out of place, her clothes were suitable for any occasion, and she was never flustered about needing to change her look for any situation. Mrs. Caplicki was like a catalog model: neat, ready, and happy.

She stood before me in the doorway wearing jeans and a light blue and white striped sweater with her hair pulled back in a ponytail. I'd never met Carla's father, but it was obvious Carla got her natural beauty and grace from her mother.

"Hi, Mrs. Caplicki," I said. "Carla told me you needed a hand with your vacuum cleaner."

"You're such a gentleman, Raymond," she said. "Thank you for coming over. I thought it was just silly to take the thing in to the repair shop. The belt slipped off again, and I don't have the strength to pull it over the spindle."

I smiled. "Did you run over a blanket again?" I couldn't count how many times she'd sucked the corner of a low-hanging blanket into the vacuum and shucked the belt off of the drive wheel.

Mrs. Caplicki sighed and smiled. "I know, I need to control where I steer that thing. Well, come on in out of the cold."

She led me into the formal living room where I spotted the accused vacuum. It stood resolutely near a couch where a bright, lilac-colored afghan spread like a giant cobweb over the cushions and then down into the business end of the vacuum on the floor. If the room had been dark, I'd swear I was looking at a black hole sucking the life out of a purple galaxy.

I laid the vacuum down and began the ministrations of extracting the blanket. It required a subtle combination of gently rocking the roller brush and giving the caught fabric a good yank now and again.

Mrs. Caplicki sat behind me in order to view the procedure, but before I'd gotten too deep into the surgery she said, "So, Raymond, how are you holding up? Carla told me about your friend."

"I'm okay," I said. "But the situation isn't what I'd call ideal."

She nodded and hugged herself. "Speaking of situations, Ray…" *Oh boy*, I thought. I should have known the vacuum was a ploy to get me over for a chat. Mrs.

Caplicki was understandably concerned about her daughter's seemingly wasted years pining for me and had hinted to me about my alleged disregard for her.

"Mrs. Caplicki, you don't need to say anything," I said. "Ever since Carla started seeing this artist guy, I've known what I need to do. I just wish now it hadn't taken me so long to realize it."

Her smile suggested she didn't believe me. Or rather, she wanted to believe me but wasn't sure if I'd follow through. I didn't blame her. "Carla won't be with him very long," she said. "She was just lonely."

I nodded apologetically and said, "I'm not very good at relationships, but I know how special she is. I'll figure it out."

Mrs. Caplicki pursed her lips, and in that instant the blanket came free of the vacuum.

As an arbiter for the most important chess tournament in the United States, Anna Krimpski came well qualified. Not only had she once been a world-class chess player with titles of Russian Women's Champion, Women's World Champion, and Gold Medalist, she also had been an arbiter at the big annual tournaments in Hastings, England; Linnares, Spain; Wik an Zee, The Netherlands, and twice at the Chess Olympiad.

As a person, Anna Krimpski had no business having a conversation with another human being.

I introduced myself to her outside the Rainier Room in the Seattle Center where play would begin in just under an hour. She wore a gray dress that hid the fact she was a woman. Her dull brown hair was pulled into a tight bun on the back of her head, counter levered by glasses with thick brown frames the size of Popsicle sticks. Her face, while oh so stern to me, had a kind of softness to it, like polished stone and looked like she may have enjoyed a touch of beauty once. Once. "I'm very busy, Mr. Gordon," she said. "I'm sure if you played chess you'd understand."

"Actually," I said with a smile, "I've been rated a Master for the past two years." Achieving Master status had been especially satisfying for me. It was one of those lifetime goals I had been able to obtain. The hard part was holding on to it.

She wasn't impressed, though. "Well, that's fine," she said. "Perhaps you can figure out on your own then how busy I am. I don't have time to speak with you right now." She turned on her heel and marched down the hall like a Nazi.

"Ms. Krimpski," I said catching up to her. "I am not Joe Reporter from some newspaper. I am trying to solve the murder of a personal friend and one of the greatest chess players of our time."

"Great? Charlie Roggenbuck?" she intoned, her nose in the air. "Maybe the amount of food he consumed was great, or the amount of money he seemed to owe, but as a chess player? Certainly not! His very name is ridiculous."

She offended me. Charlie had taught me a lot. "Ms. Krimpski, I must…"

"Are you a police officer, Mr. Gordon?" she asked, cutting me off and accenting 'Mr.' in a tone that belonged on a women's talk show.

"No, I am not," I said.

"Then I am under no obligation to speak with you. Is that correct?"

"It is."

"Goodbye, Mr. Gordon."

She did it. I knew it. Her evil oozed like a stain. I could imagine Charlie cowering under the witch as she socked him with her broomstick. If Anna Krimpski was the last person Charlie saw as he died, he had probably welcomed death with open arms.

14

☐ I don't know if my staying to watch the next round of the tournament irritated Anna Krimpski or not. I hoped so, but she never seemed to look in my direction.

During a chess tournament, each opponent was given a specific amount of time to play the game. At this US Chess Championship, each player was given one hundred minutes to complete his or her first forty moves. Fifty minutes would then be added to work through the next twenty moves, then ten minutes for the rest of the game. If those requirements were not met, the player would lose the game. If one player was checkmated or resigned before those time limits, which often happened, the game would be over as well.

A special clock with two faces kept time. When it was White's move, his clock was ticking while Black's was not. When White finished his move, he pushed a button on the clock, stopping his timer and starting Black's. People who didn't play chess might not understand that the amount of mental energy spent on strategy, tactics, and calculation was tremendous for a chess player, but we all knew how stressful it was to be under the weight of time.

After I'd been watching the tournament for two hours, Vladimir Penski came and sat next to me. His face was long and sallow, his eyes were red, and he walked heavily, slowly. I glanced at the tournament board; he'd just lost to David McKay, a Master from New York.

I gave Vladimir a sympathetic smile as he sat down and sighed. McKay was one of the lower rated players, more in my league than Vladimir's. Penski was rated sixth highest in the tournament. A draw wouldn't have been unusual, but a full loss? I couldn't say anything to him. He slumped his shoulders and stared ahead, his mind elsewhere, his furry eyebrows bunched in thought.

"Vladimir," I said quietly, "how about I buy you a beer tonight? I could use some company."

"I think I will need something with more kick than beer," he said.

There was a sudden commotion at a table just in front of us. Ben Davis was on his feet and mumbling to himself. He paced back and forth while staring at the table and shaking his head. He was short and stocky, maybe even pudgy, but still a possible physical threat to his opponent, Elena Johnson. She was in her thirties and most of the male players had a crush on her, but if Ben got violent for some reason...

I saw both arbiters, Graham Saunders and Anna Krimpski, eyeing the situation but neither made a move until Ben started stabbing his finger at Elena. Graham was at the far side of the room and started moving but was too late. Ben laid his arm on the table and swept the chess pieces off, scattering them like marbles on the floor. Players ignored their clocks and turned to see what was happening. Elena sat still, her face a work of stone until Ben threw up his arms with a groan and stalked out of the room. Then she sighed and closed her eyes.

The playing hall was silent; everyone looked at Graham Saunders and Anna Krimpski who were nose-to-nose and whispering furiously. They were the arbiters, but to me it seemed like Ben's action was clearly a resignation. Outbursts like that were unheard of, and everyone wanted to know what had happened and what it meant for the rest of the tournament. Would he be disqualified? Censured somehow? We all waited silently.

Then I heard a soft tap. And another.

Elena Johnson had collected the pieces from the floor and was sitting at her table putting them back into the position they'd been in before Ben swept them away. She probably should have left them alone. Just like a crime scene where the police want to see it uncontaminated so they can uncover any evidence as it was left behind, Nigel Cross would want to see the chess pieces strewn about, but she seemed determined to put them back.

I watched as she methodically placed the pieces in the center of their respective squares. The two Kings, then a Rook, then a Bishop, another Rook, and a series of pawns. Exactly where they were before the disruption. Then Elena reached across the chessboard and tipped over Ben's King. I guessed she decided Ben had resigned, too.

15

☐ "I'm sorry, Vladimir," I said as I stood, "we might have to get that drink tomorrow night."

I'd never seen anyone lose control at a chess tournament like Ben Davis had. His outburst needed to be looked into because if he had a history of explosive anger issues... I could only wonder if he got upset while playing Charlie in the hotel room. I wanted to leave Seattle Center though, so no one would discover who I was checking up on. Besides, it helped me concentrate on the task at hand.

Instead of driving home, I stopped at the first comfortable restaurant I came across, a little place on 6th Avenue full of ferns and purple chairs. I ordered a latte, opened my laptop, and logged onto the almighty Internet.

According to the US Open online roster, Ben Davis made his home in New Mexico and frequented most of the chess tournaments in Texas and California. I'd seen him at some of those events but never struck up a conversation. I'd also played him at the Chicago Open a few years before, and he'd beaten me pretty handily in a Dragon variation of the Sicilian defense. He'd been quiet, never left the table, and afterword shook my hand with a curt single pump.

Which meant absolutely nothing. A shy unassuming chess player was not unique. Most of the people I knew could fit that description, but not all of them had erupted like Mt. St. Helens when his chess game didn't go his way. What was the significance?

But there was little more to find about Ben Davis. He was a chess player was about all I could verify. He had no personal web site or blogs—at least not under his name—there were no discussion groups or devoted fan sites or anti-Ben Davis sites for that matter. None of the New Mexico police departments listed him as an outstanding criminal, and there was nothing about him being wanted by any other law enforcement agency. The only place I could find the name Ben Davis was on the United States Chess Federation website where he was listed as the number one player from New Mexico. And I found nothing about emotional instability.

What was the connection? What was I missing? Davis swept the pieces from the board and stalked out and then Elena put the pieces back…

She'd toppled the King!

Maybe *she* killed Charlie. I laughed out loud. How absurd would it be if Elena had actually shot Charlie and this was how she was discovered? I laughed out loud again and heard someone behind me clear their throat in a you-know-you're-in-public-don't-you sort of way. It was remarkable, crazy even, for me to even think it. Had I found Charlie's murderer by pure luck? No way, I thought, and shook my head. What possibly could have been her motive? Of course, I didn't have any idea what the motive behind Charlie's murder was anyway so really, there was no reason to believe it couldn't have been Elena Johnson or Ben Davis.

I grabbed my coat and laptop and raced back to the Seattle Center. I needed to talk to Elena before the next round started. I'd been looking at a computer for answers; maybe it was time I talked to a real person who might be able to give me some insight.

The doors were open, and a few of the players were outside smoking; some were talking with one another, and I saw a couple with newspapers. I wormed my way through and made it inside without a word from anyone. According to the results on the wall chart, the arbiters had ruled Ben Davis's outburst a resignation and awarded a full win to Elena. No surprise there.

While I scanned the chart for the games prior to Charlie's death, looking to see who had lost to him, someone who might hold a grudge, the sound around me flattened, and I lost track of the ambient noise filtering in through the doors. I glanced over my shoulder and saw Elena Johnson standing behind me.

She, too, was looking at the results of the day's rounds. She was about five feet seven and stood confidently but unthreateningly. Her dark hair was pulled into a ponytail, and while she wasn't drop dead gorgeous, there was something statuesque about her, like whatever she was looking at had her absolute attention.

I looked back at the chart and saw that Ben Davis had lost to Charlie in the first round of play. Would he have killed over the loss of a game? No other chess players he'd lost to had been found murdered at past tournaments. What was different about this one?

I was just about to ask Elena Johnson what she knew about Ben Davis when a voice I didn't want to hear called my name.

"Ray Gordon," he called again, louder. Everyone in the room turned to see Detective John Keller, his partner Mark Peters, and four uniformed cops standing by the door. Then they all looked at me.

My stomach sank as if I had just stepped off the Space Needle. Keller was up to something and wanted to embarrass me. He brought the uniforms for show. "He's right there officers," Keller said, pointing at me. "Raymond Gordon," he said as one of the uniforms cuffed my wrists behind my back, "you're under arrest for the murder of Charles Roggenbuck."

16

☐ My single phone call was to Carla Caplicki. Not only did she know me better than anyone else, but as a county employee, she knew a few lawyers. Some she knew because of her job with the Treasurer's Office where she helped land-owning attorneys with their tax and property issues, but mostly she knew them from chitchat in and around the halls and offices of the King County courthouse. Carla told me she knew just the guy and would give him a call.

For an hour and a half, I sat silently in a generic interrogation room with an equally blank uniformed guard who stood against the wall like a tree. It gave me time to think about everything that had happened.

Nigel Cross claimed Charlie might have been cheating which I really couldn't believe. Charlie cheating at chess was an abomination, unnatural like truth in politics. What I did know was that Charlie played outside the tournaments. It wasn't cheating, but during big tournaments it might be considered unethical to play someone you might get paired against in the next round or two. Ben Davis obviously had a temper and needed to be looked into. Elena Johnson had knocked over the King. That was weak, but I thought worth looking into, and then the whole idea of some of the pieces being wiped down for fingerprints got me thinking about someone else.

Before I could complete my thought, the door opened and Carla peered around the side before she stepped inside. She stared at the floor with hunched shoulders like a teenager applying for her first job. Her hand hovered above the empty chair across from me and she glanced at the guard. He dropped his chin an inch and she sat down. "Ray, what's going on?" she whispered.

"Idiocy run amok. Spite. Not knowing how to properly investigate a murder." I shrugged. "Take your pick."

Carla leaned over the table, her hands still in her lap. "If they think you did it, why haven't they talked to me? I was with you."

"Because John Keller has no idea what's going on. He wanted it to be a nice tidy suicide but that got thrown out. He asked me what I thought, and now he needs to make a show for his captain. Arresting me did that and allowed him to embarrass me."

The door swung inward again, and Carla clamped her lips together and slid back in her seat. A man I didn't recognize entered the room followed by Keller who made a point to shut the door with a solid *thunk* and remained there. He nodded at the guard and hitched his pants. *Did he really just do that?* I asked myself. I rolled my eyes.

The first man through the door set a briefcase on the table and then sat next to it, one foot on the floor, the other dangling. There was nothing extraordinary about him. He was of average height and build, brown hair and eyes, no glasses, no birthmarks, tattoos or outstanding peculiarities. He wore a light blue button up dress shirt that was open at the collar, no tie, and black slacks that ended in spectacularly glassy obsidian shoes. He looked like he'd just gotten home from the office and was just sitting down with a beer before getting called down to the police station. "Hi," he said shaking my hand, "I'm Dan Hennesy. Carla filled me in as much as she could. What have you told them?"

"I haven't told them anything," I said. "Detective Keller here has very poor manners as well as a mean streak, so it makes no sense to talk to him."

"So I've heard," Dan said, not missing a beat. I liked him instantly.

Keller's face reddened as he shot a look at my new lawyer. "What's that supposed to mean?" he said. "Who's been saying...?"

"I'm sorry, Detective," Dan said, "but I'm trying to have a private conversation with my client. He seems to have been arrested under false pretenses. Would you please excuse us?"

John's already red face deepened in hue, and he stalked out of the room followed by the mute guard.

"So what's this guy's problem, Ray?" Hennesy asked.

I told him about our unfortunate pairing on the Seattle P.D. and how he thought I'd gotten away with murder. "And he still hates you I see," Dan said.

"Can you believe it? Some partner." I sighed and sat back. "No need to dig up the past."

"On the contrary. We might be able to use his dislike for you. The charges against you are laughable. It's harassment, plain and simple."

"What's he got on me?"

"Well, before I came in here I was able to look through their case," he said as he popped the locks on his briefcase and pulled out a legal pad inked over with scribbled notes. "Detective Keller seems to think you're jealous of your old friend's success, and you're using your knowledge of police work to cover your tracks. He believes you went there earlier to commit the murder and then came back with Carla to create the illusion of finding the body. You already admitted to having a meeting scheduled with this Roggenbuck fellow and an employee of the hotel recognized your photo."

"Who recognized me?" I asked.

Dan searched his notes. "A Victoria Brown. She said you asked directions to Roggenbuck's room."

I smiled and looked at Carla. She wasn't amused. I shrugged and thought for a moment. "So I was right. John's getting pressure from the brass, and he arrested me based on flimsy evidence so it would look like he was actually doing something. I know more about this case than the police do!"

Dan shrugged. "I'll start drawing up a suit against them."

"Don't bother. I don't want to sue the Seattle Police Department."

"Mr. Gordon. My God. You were publicly arrested among your peers for no reason. He went out of his way to humiliate you. That's blatantly and fantastically wrong!"

"Ray," Carla pleaded, "you might want to think about this."

I nodded. "John Keller is an ass. No doubt. But the entire police department doesn't need to get dragged into court because they made a mistake in hiring him. We can clear my name, ask for an apology, but that's all. No lawsuit."

Dan shrugged again, this time with pursed lips.

"Hand me a piece of paper and a pen, will you," I said.

He slid the yellow legal pad to me and I tore a strip of paper and wrote two sentences on it then folded it into a small square. I slid the pad back to Dan. "Did you call the Youth Center for me?" I asked Carla.

"Yes. I let them know you couldn't make it today."

"Thanks. So when can we get out of here?" I asked, looking back at my attorney.

"Right now. I had you out before I walked into this room," he said.

"Carla was right. You're the best," I said with a smile.

"Excuse me, Ray, but am I privy to your little note there?"

"Nope."

17

☐ While my visit with the police had been shorter than if I'd actually been a criminal, it had nevertheless stolen a total of three hours from my own investigation—unofficial as it was. And it made me want a shower. Three hours in a cop car and an interrogation room is nerve-wracking and just a bit stressful—even with the best lawyer in Seattle sitting in the chair beside me.

"Thanks for helping Mom," Carla said as she drove me back to my car. "She called and said you were the best, as usual."

I wanted to ask what they really talked about, but instead I shrugged and said, "What can I say, your mom knows talent."

Carla smiled. "Whatever. It's nice of you to go is all. Thank you."

"It's no problem. It's the least I could do for the mother of my lawyer connection. Can I buy you dinner to say thanks?"

Carla shook her head. "I've got plans tonight," she said.

I interpreted that as a date with the artist. I stared at her, but I had no right to be upset. "Maybe next time?" I asked.

"Maybe."

Carla dropped me off at my car, and I thanked her for the ride. She beeped her horn as she drove away, and I wondered if the things she'd said, things I thought were invitations of sorts, were just my imagination. Was I jealous of the guy Carla was seeing? Yes, I couldn't deny it. Carla had been my friend for so long, had always been there for me, and now... But that was it. What was I to her? I knew she'd wanted to take our relationship to the next level, and I always resisted. Why? My parents had been ripped from my life when I was a kid. I'd seen the shrinks and cried the tears. Carla wasn't a parent, and she'd been around longer than them. What the hell was wrong with me?

I shook my head and sighed. As much as I didn't want to see Carla unhappy, I hoped the artist would turn out to be a flake.

When I got home, I abandoned the car in the driveway and ran to the front of the house. My five-by-nine picture window had been smashed. Some of the glass was still intact, suspended from the top like a guillotine, some standing upright at the bottom like a deadly line of crystalline stalagmites. The flowerbed under the window was barely littered with shards so something must have gone through the window and carried the big broken slabs with it. Probably scared Morphy half to…

Morphy! He usually barked when I came home.

I fought the key into the lock and pushed through the front door. "Morphy!" I called. "Morphy?"

He was a pile of fur on the floor in front of the couch. He flopped his tail a couple of times at the sight of me but didn't make a sound. He looked up at me like a beggar lying against a dusty broken wall, holding his cup out. He had to be weak. There was a lot of blood.

I knelt down and put my hand in front of his nose. Somewhere I'd read it was the thing to do so your dog had a familiar and comfortable scent during a time of duress.

With my other hand, I gingerly pushed and probed a long bloody gash from his right shoulder down to the elbow. I didn't want to move him if there was glass in the wound.

Twice I made him yelp from my lack of medical training, but I couldn't find any sign of glass or anything else in the wound. I took off my flannel shirt and balled it up under his head and ran into the bathroom. I grabbed four towels and ran back into the living room where I kicked a brick that happened to be lying in the middle of the floor.

The strange thing was my first thought, why would I leave a brick on the floor, or why would I even have a lone brick inside the house? There were no masonry projects on my agenda, no loose bricks in the fireplace…then I remembered why it was so cold in the house and that my dog was bleeding to death.

I loosely folded one towel like a compress and put it on top of Morphy's wound. Then I wrapped another towel around his neck and shoulder and tied it down to keep the first "bandage" in place. The other two towels I simply used as blankets to keep him warm.

I jammed the brick against the door to prop it open then ran for the car. I drove it over my lawn and lurched to a stop so the passenger door aligned with the front stoop. I jogged back inside, hoisted Morphy up as slowly as I could. When he whimpered, my eyes flooded and I choked on my words. "I'm taking care of you, pal. Don't worry, you'll be okay." Please, God, let him be okay, I prayed.

Once Morphy was packed into the passenger seat with the extra towels secured around him, I leapt behind the wheel and stepped on the gas. I dug two black scars across my lawn, hopped onto the street and raced for the vet.

The drive was a blur. There was a lot of honking, some swearing, and a complete disregard for turn signals. I kept one hand on Morphy at all times to keep him from sliding out of the seat when we went around corners.

We bounced into the parking lot of Morphy's veterinarian, and I ran inside screaming for help. A doctor and two assistants almost tackled me and asked what had happened. It took me a beat to realize I was covered with Morphy's blood, and they thought I was hurt. "Not me," I yelled. "My dog. He's in the car!"

They wheeled Morphy from outside on a dog-sized gurney and pushed him through a door. The receptionist grabbed my elbow and guided me back to where they'd taken him. While the doctors gave Morph a quick exam, someone asked me questions about what had happened. Everything was happening at once, I don't remember what I told them. After a few minutes Morphy disappeared around a corner, and I was escorted back to the waiting room.

I heaved a deep breath and sank into the vinyl seats in the waiting area. It seemed like hours, even days. Where was Morphy? He had to be scared. I dredged up our trips to the beach where he would charge a flock of seagulls and scatter them into the wind. He'd casually watch them circle and land behind him, and then after a few steps in the opposite direction he'd turn around and bound after them again. Sometimes he'd launch himself into the water as a small wave rolled in over the sand and he'd leap up and down in the water like a little boy playing in a puddle.

My best friend was dying somewhere in a back room all alone. I wiped my eyes and choked back a sob.

I stood and paced the length of the vet's sterile office. The floor was white vinyl and there were stacks of a special brand of dog food—not available in stores I guessed—and there were a few worn *Cat Fancy* magazines on the table. I rolled my eyes and borrowed a phone book from the heavy eyed assistant behind the counter. I called someone to replace the glass in my window and then went outside and looked at the brick that had been thrown through it. After I'd gotten Morphy into the Land Cruiser, I had gone back to close the door of the house and noticed something had been scratched into the offending brick. At the time it made little sense, so I tossed it in the backseat thinking I'd look at it later.

Later was at the vet's while Morphy was fighting for his life on the operating table. The message on the brick still made little sense. "Thanks a lot" was scratched into the surface. Maybe it was meant as a sarcastic note from the person who'd actually killed Charlie thanking me for taking the rap. Or perhaps it was from one of the chess players who thought I killed Charlie thanks to my public arrest by Detective John Keller, thanking me—again, sarcastically—for taking away a friend and colleague? I dropped the brick onto the floorboards and sat down with the door open.

I needed to think. If Detective Keller wasn't doing anything about finding Charlie Roggenbuck's killer, he should have let me.

I'd lost three hours in the police station. During that time, I could have been talking with other players like Elena Johnson or even to Ben Davis if he'd shown his face yet. I could have tried to discover if he'd killed Charlie. And if he had, why? More importantly I might have been home and my dog, my friend and best buddy, wouldn't be in the surgery room.

Why had Ben Davis erupted at the tournament? That was the first question that needed to be answered. If Ben was just a hothead and threw temper tantrums, fine. But if the pressure of having just murdered a man was getting to him then he was ready to either snap in half like a dry stick of kindling, in which case he might confess, or he would kill again in order to protect himself if necessary. But where was he? I wanted to talk to him alone. The tournament site offered too many distractions, too many places to run if he said anything incriminating.

There were hundreds of hotels in the greater Seattle area, and I was sure many of the players were staying with friends or family. Where was Ben Davis? The tournament director probably had a list of where all the players were staying and how they could be reached. I thought it would be easy enough to find out where Nigel Cross kept that list and "borrow" it just long enough to see where Mr. Davis was spending his evenings. Or, in order to save myself some potential embarrassment or more time in a jail cell, I thought it might be better to just follow Davis after the next round of play.

My next move then, was to talk to Elena Johnson. It was a crazy notion to even think of her killing Charlie simply because she tipped over a King after the game had ended, but she may have noticed some odd behavior about Ben Davis during their match or even beforehand and I was sure Keller hadn't given her a thought. If she did know something, she might be more willing to talk about it since her scare with Davis. I already knew where she was staying, too, because all of the male players knew and liked to brag that they knew. Elena was the dream girl of most chess players who found themselves entered in the same tournament as her. She had the looks and she played chess. What else could be asked of a woman? So with immature abandon and glee, several of the more technically savvy players tried to be the first to obtain Elena's hotel arrangements and then brag about who found her first. Childish? Yes, but useful for me. Elena Johnson was staying at the Sheraton Hotel on 6th Avenue.

I'd already looked up the number and was poised to call her when my cell phone rang. It was Deacon Kamalov from the St. Nicholas Russian Orthodox Church. "Nice to hear from you, Father. Do you have news for me?"

"You don't sound very happy, Mr. Gordon. Is everything all right?" he asked.

"Actually, no. My dog is in the hospital."

"Oh, I'm sorry to hear that. I hope he'll be okay. But, yes, I do have some news for you." Deacon Kamalov's English was excellent, only an occasional Slavic pronunciation gave away his heritage. "The woman you asked about came and picked up the note from Mr. Druga this morning. I tried to reach you earlier but you never answered."

"Sorry Father. I've been detained most of the day. Can you tell me her full name?"

"That's why I needed to speak with you. I'm afraid you're looking for the wrong person."

"Why do you say that?" I asked.

"I've known Sara for several years now as she is a regular member of our congregation. Sara has no children."

"I know, Father," I said. "Her baby died."

"I'm sorry Mr. Gordon, but she insists she's never been a mother."

"But she took the note?"

"Yes."

"Then she obviously knows something. Someone is lying."

Nothing made any sense. I went back inside the vet's and after a half hour was told Morphy would need to spend the night. He'd lost a lot of blood, and they'd "know more" in the morning.

I got in the car and dialed Carla. She didn't pick up, and I remembered she had plans for the night. I decided not to leave a message and drove home, slowly since I couldn't see the road through the blur. And it wasn't even raining.

18

☐ There was a new window in my living room wall when I arrived, and from the outside, everything looked normal. I even smiled at the speed of the glass shop's service, but the aftermath of what had happened was still inside and eroded my mood as soon as I opened the door. The floor and couch in front of the window were minefields of broken glass and stained with Morphy's blood. I picked up the larger shards and then found my vacuum to suck up what I couldn't see before tackling the bloodstains.

As I blotted and scrubbed the carpet, I wondered if Charlie's mistress/lover/girlfriend/whatever had lied about the pregnancy. It obviously wasn't about money since she left him while he was in Europe. Was it a ploy to entice Charlie into marriage? Or was this a different Sara? Tony said he'd never met her. What could an imposter's angle be?

I placed Sara in the second person to find slot on my mental list and called the Sheraton on 6th. Elena Johnson wasn't answering her phone. I chose not to leave a message since she'd watched from close range when I was ceremoniously arrested. I'd call later to see if she was there and then show up at the door.

I reminded myself I was going to speak with her about Ben Davis. I'd bring up the King incident, but there really wasn't much to it as a theory.

Charlie's King had been tipped over in resignation. Charlie Roggenbuck rarely resigned a game of chess. There were very few recorded instances of him giving up in a major tournament. He was a fighter to the end. I sat at my chess table again, the pieces still set up with Charlie's final game.

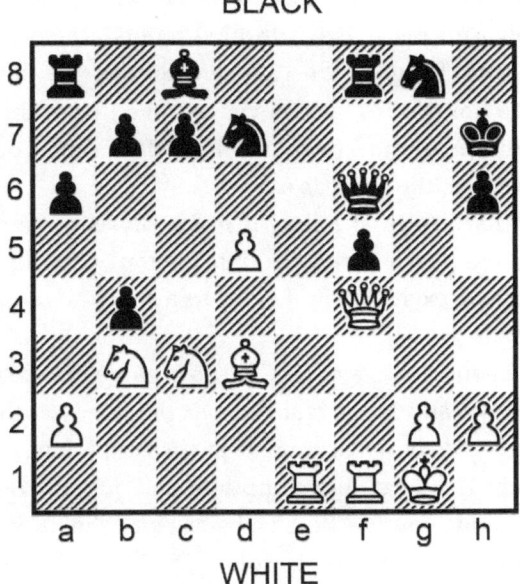

I was confident the move for white was Rook to e6, threatening the Black Queen. Black would respond by moving the Queen to c3, capturing the sacrificed White Knight. From that point, White would continue to attack, using his Bishop to capture the pawn on f5 and placing the Black King in check.

If Black moved his King to safety, White could swarm the area and either checkmate the King or win enough material to obtain a decidedly superior advantage. So Black must capture the Bishop with his Rook. White would win the piece exchange by then capturing the Rook with his Queen.

While point systems aren't used in chess, the pieces themselves are given a value as a way of determining their strengths on the board. For example, the Queen, as the most powerful piece, is worth nine points. Rooks are five, Bishops and Knights are each worth three, and pawns equal one point. Kings are never removed from the board and therefore are not given a point value. When the King is checkmated, the game is over.

In Charlie's final game, if my analysis were correct, winning the Black Rook for his Bishop, Charlie would have won the exchange and enjoyed a small advantage. So why resign?

I'd been looking over Charlie's game for nearly an hour when I suddenly realized *my* picture was the only one Keller had shown around at the Westin Hotel.

Again, I sat at my computer and logged onto the Internet and found the website for the US Chess Championship. I made a color print of all sixty-five players and then left my house again for downtown Seattle.

Traffic was light, and I made it to the Westin Hotel in less than twenty minutes. The lovely young woman I now knew as Victoria Brown was again behind the front desk. I slowed my pace as my heartbeat increased. She was wearing the same hotel uniform of skirt, blouse and tie I'd seen her in before and her hair was pulled back in a ponytail again, tied with a purple ribbon. I wondered what Carla would look like in the same clothing and if she'd have the same smile. I gave myself a mental headshake. Where was I going with ideas like that?

I stopped and looked for the manager's office. It was at the far end of the lobby, and I started walking toward it.

"Hey, I know you!" It was Victoria Brown. I stopped and looked. "Will you come over here and tell me what's going on?"

"I wish I knew," I said walking over to her.

She smirked. "You're involved somehow. You were here the night one of our guests died."

"Aren't you afraid I did it?"

She tilted her head and smiled with a 'I knew you were going to ask that' look. "No, because the police asked about you and said they knew where you were. Since you're here and not in jail…" She shrugged.

"Here I am," I said. "Did the detective you spoke with show you any of these faces?" I asked and fanned the pictures of the chess players I'd printed out on the counter.

Ms. Brown picked up the sheaf of paper and gave each player a once over. "Are you a policeman?" she asked, her eyes still on the pages.

"Retired," I said.

"Oh my God," she said.

"What?"

"Were you shot or something?"

"No. Why?"

"You're way too young to be retired."

I smiled and my face felt hot. "It's a long story," I said, focusing again on the credit card applications I'd seen when I'd first met Miss Victoria Brown.

She smiled and began scanning the pictures again. "Maybe you can tell me sometime," she said. "Oh, here's one."

"Here's one what?" I asked, thankful for the timely change of subject.

Women weren't exactly a phobia of mine as much as a kind of giddy fear. My social life was a derailed train full of clammy hands, mumbled hellos, embarrassed smiles, and an "aw shucks" type of reaction to any attention given me. I blamed it on some sort of childhood affliction I'd missed an immunization for. Nothing else could really explain it.

"I recognize this man," Victoria said, turning the page so I could see it.

"Ben Davis," I said. "Where have you seen him?"

"I can't tell you."

"What? Why not?"

Victoria put a practiced smile on. "Good evening, sir. How may I help you?"

I got it. Customer confidentiality. Ben Davis was staying at the Westin Hotel. "Thank you. You've been very helpful," I said.

"My name's Victoria," she said and pointed to her name tag.

"I know. I'm Ray Gordon."

"I know," she said.

I smiled and walked toward the door. When I was out of Victoria's sight I found a lobby phone and hit zero. When the hotel operator answered, I asked for Ben Davis.

He wasn't there.

19

Seattle's Sheraton Hotel sat on 6th Avenue and boasted a view of some of Seattle's best shopping. To the north was Nike Town where anything with the swoosh could be found; to the west was FAO Schwartz and City Centre, an upscale mall; and just up the street was the Convention Center complete with a glass canopy that covered the street and protected conventioneers from Seattle's famous bouts of cool rain. Not coincidentally, bookstores, delis, antique shops, fashion stores, and boutiques were all within a few steps.

It was just after ten p.m. when I walked into the lobby and showed my stack of photos to the concierge, a skinny young man with red hair and freckles who could have been mistaken for a scarecrow in another setting. "Elena Johnson is a guest here," I said showing him her picture. "I need to speak with her immediately." The revelation that Ben Davis was staying at the same hotel as Charlie had triggered the alarm bells in my head. If he had indeed murdered Charlie, for whatever reason, Elena Johnson could be in just as much danger based on Davis's outburst at the tournament.

"Are you with the police?" he asked.

"No. I'm conducting an unofficial investigation into the murder of one of her colleagues though."

"I see," he said crisply. He couldn't have been older than twenty-seven, but his professionalism was solid. I admired that; protect the guests of the hotel. Victoria Brown had done the same thing at the Westin. He glanced past me and with an almost imperceptible nod brought the manager to my elbow. His gold-plated name badge identified him as Roger.

"May I help you, Mr...?" he asked.

"Gordon. My name's Ray Gordon. Don't worry. I'm not trying to break any rules. I need to speak with Elena Johnson. You can either escort me to her room or I'll wait right here for you to bring her down. Either way is fine with me."

"May I ask what this is all about?" Roger the Manager asked.

"A friend of mine was murdered a few days ago. She might know something about it."

"Are you a police officer?"

"No. I'm an ex-cop trying to do some private detective work because...well, let's just say I'm not brimming with confidence when it comes to the way the case is being handled by the authorities. Now will you please just call her and let her know I want to speak with her?"

Roger the Manager adjusted his tie and looked at the concierge, who made another imperceptible gesture. "One moment please," he said.

I stood my ground and flipped through the photos while he stepped behind the counter with the concierge and picked up the telephone. After holding the receiver to his ear for a minute or two he hung up. "I'm sorry, Mr. Gordon. Miss Johnson must not be in."

"How many times did it ring?" I asked.

"A dozen."

I checked my watch. It was almost ten thirty p.m. There was no law against staying out late, but I knew chess players. During a major tournament, no one was hitting the bars. "We need to get to her room," I said.

Roger the Manager held up both hands to calm me down. "Mr. Gordon, our guests are entitled to their privacy. If they choose not to answer the phone, there's nothing I can do."

"Exactly. I'm looking into a murder. I want to make sure she still has the ability to choose."

"Mr. Crawford," the concierge said. "He checks out. The police department lists Ray Gordon as having retired several years ago."

I whirled around and stared at the kid behind the desk. "Who'd you call?" I asked.

He smiled without showing any teeth. "I have a friend at the police station," he said. "She works late."

Roger the Manager, now Mr. Roger Crawford, nodded his head. "Thank you. All right Mr. Gordon. Come with me." He led me around the corner to the elevator lobby. Inside the car he pressed the button for the seventeenth floor. "This is highly unusual," he said.

"I'm sure it is, Mr. Crawford. It's just that there was an incident today and I'm worried about her. I certainly don't want to step on anyone's toes here, but a murder investigation is never pleasant—for anyone involved."

"I have no doubt that's true, but I want you to understand you're only here because I'm now concerned for the safety of one of my guests. You're only along because Mr. Kirkpatrick, our concierge, had the forethought to check your credentials."

I nodded and glanced at the floor register. I thought about getting Mr. Kirkpatrick a thank you gift then wondered again who he'd talked to at the police department.

The doors slid open, and a pair of women looking to be in their forties and dressed like they wanted to be in their twenties twittered between us as we exited the elevator. Their miniskirts and tight neon tops jiggled with each high-heeled step. "Good evening, ladies," Roger the Manager said with a smile.

"Hi ya, hon," they said in unison and then burst into giggles. Mercifully, the doors slid shut.

"This way," Crawford said.

The door to room 1702 was closed and locked. After two minutes of unanswered door pounding Crawford produced a master key card and swiped it through the electronic lock. "Miss Johnson?" he called as he pushed open the door. "My name is Roger Crawford. I'm the hotel manager. I'm coming inside. Are you here, Miss Johnson?"

I stood in the hallway as Crawford inched his way inside the dark room. I put a toe forward to keep the door open. Crawford flipped on a light, and I waited for him to call me but there was nothing. I nudged the door open until I could see him standing inside, his back to me and his finger still on the light switch.

"Roger?" I said. He didn't move. I took two steps and looked over his shoulder. Elena Johnson lay sprawled face down on the bed. Her head and hands were hanging over the end as if she were looking for something, but the pool of blood she seemed to be staring down at wasn't coming from under the bed.

20

☐ "This is turning into some little hobby for you, isn't it, Ray?" John Keller said, as he strode down the hallway and stopped just inches in front of me. His breath was like a stale summer day behind a cannery.

"I know it's late, John, and you've had such a busy day, but keeping some mints handy wouldn't be a bad thing."

"You want to play it funny, huh?" he said smugly, though he did take a step back. "How about I haul you down to the station again? This is the second body you've found. Those statistics are looking pretty good."

I crossed my arms and stared back. Until recently, it had been a long time since I'd seen John. With that distance between us, I would have thought being around him again wouldn't make me so angry, but I was wrong. Maybe it was the way he was handling Charlie's case. I took a deep breath and cleared my head. "I don't want to keep fighting with you, Detective," I said, "but the truth of the matter is, if you wouldn't have arrested me, Elena Johnson might still be alive." I tried to hold my temper but the irritation I felt toward John at that moment spread quickly. "Did you even bother to look into the other players in the tournament?" I asked. "No? Try this one; Ben Davis, who went slightly crazy during this morning's round, is staying at the Westin. Remember that hotel, John? That's where the first body was found. And by the way, the person Ben Davis was playing when he freaked out is now lying dead inside this room. Did you try to find any other leads besides the fact that I was going to visit the deceased?

"I would greatly appreciate it if you did some police work *before* making accusations." Before he had time to think of a response, I pushed past him, stomped out the door and stood with my back against the opposite wall in the hallway, out from underfoot of the forensics team moving in and out of the room. I breathed deep and smelled the blood in the air.

As I hoped he would, Keller got frustrated and ordered his partner to question me. He ducked inside Elena Johnson's room, and Mark Peters loomed toward me like a great shadow stretched across a wall. "Well good evening, Detective Peters," I said. "How did my hunch play out?"

Peters glanced over his shoulder and then said, "I had a couple of uniforms pick him up, and I was just finishing up my questions with him when we got this call."

The note I'd written in the company of my lawyer had gone discreetly to Detective Peters via the desk sergeant at the police department. The idea of only some of Charlie's chess pieces being wiped down had bothered me ever since Keller had told me about it. Then I remembered who I'd seen the first day I visited the tournament site. Ryan Brooks was an outstanding chess player capable of giving Charlie Roggenbuck a fight for the title. And he was a junk food junkie. He ate chips and cheese puffs to the point his fingertips were encased in powdery, artificially flavored orange residue. My note had asked Detective Peters to ask Ryan about his whereabouts the evening of Charlie's death.

"Did he tell you anything?" I asked.

Peters nodded. "He said we already arrested the killer."

"Meaning me."

Another nod. "Right. But he's hiding something. He's very twitchy, no eye contact. Like that."

"Did you let him go?"

"No way. Not when he's acting buggy. I'll talk to him some more when we get back. John likes to do the paperwork on our calls, so it'll give me some alone time with him."

"John likes the paperwork?" I asked.

Peters shrugged. "He thinks it will get him noticed."

I shook my head. "Can I get in on your time with Ryan?"

"You know you can't, Ray," he said, "but you can watch and listen in."

"Okay. I'll meet you…"

Keller emerged from the room and caught me chatting up Detective Peters as if we were old buddies. I clammed up and took a step away from his partner. "What is it with chess players?" Keller said. "The papers will have a field day with this. Two contenders for the

Championship both found murdered, probably by a colleague not good enough to have made the cut. Is that about right, Ray?"

I nodded. "Yeah, I'd say that about sums it up."

Keller snorted. "So was she playing a game with someone too? I see a chess board in there."

I shrugged and looked up at Peters. He shrugged back.

John stared at his partner for a few seconds, passed his gaze over me, and said, "Okay. Well, it looks like she was shot in the head," Keller said. His voice quieted to something more complacent rather than the belligerence he'd started with. "From point blank range. We haven't found any casings, just like at the Roggenbuck scene and the shots were in and out. Forensics found shell fragments there. I'm sure they'll find some here as well, and then we can run a ballistics match."

Peters and I nodded at him. I wondered why John was offering up his information in my presence. Maybe it was because I didn't argue with him, or maybe he was caught off guard by seeing Peters and me talking. Maybe the carnage inside Elena's room had suddenly softened him, or maybe he wanted me to take the lead in his investigation again. Who knew?

"Are you going to take me off the list of suspects now Detective?" I asked. "Oh wait. That's right, I'm your only suspect, right? I must be very sneaky to have shot her while you were wasting my time in jail."

"All right, Gordon. No need to be smug. I've got a case to solve."

"Yeah, you do, but you're a little too late getting started. Here's your list of suspects," I said and jammed the rolled-up sheets of paper into his stomach. "Starting with the guy on top would be a really good idea. In the meantime, we'll talk to Ryan Brooks before he gets cut loose."

Oops.

21

☐ Detectives Keller and Peters moved down the hall where I couldn't hear. John's arms moved fast, up and down like a college basketball coach. He pointed at Peters, he pointed at me, he turned and started to walk away but turned back. Peters held his ground with a nod or shake of his head, and he shrugged his shoulders once. John was understandably upset at not knowing about Ryan Brooks being brought in for questioning, but my guess was he was even more pissed off because I'd asked Peters to bring him in and he did.

"So, what's with this Brooks kid?" John asked when they returned from their private conversation. "What's his involvement in this?"

"He's one of the chess players in the tournament," I said. I told him about my theory of the wiped down chess pieces in Charlie's room.

"You think he may have popped Roggenbuck?" Keller asked.

"I have no idea, John."

"How about the woman in there?" he said jabbing his thumb toward Elena Johnson's open door. "You believe she may have done it? Is that it?"

I shrugged. "Anything's possible at this point. Since she's been shot, too, maybe she was hired to kill him, if you really want to take stabs in the dark. The first rule of assassination is to kill the assassin. She was obviously involved somehow."

"Why would someone hire her to kill someone?" Keller asked. He put the emphasis on *her* as if she would be unable to do the job.

I shook my head and studied the ceiling for a moment. "John, I was just throwing crap out there. I was trying to make a point that anything is possible."

He stared at me and worked his jaw. "It might make sense, though, if it was a professional hit. Roggenbuck's murder that is, because of his gambling debts."

I moved my hands out in front of me to catch my jaw before it hit the floor. He'd actually asked someone else questions about Charlie Roggenbuck. I felt a little guilty about snapping at him but it seemed we were on a roll so I let it pass. "Possibly. I don't know anything about Charlie owing money." Granted, Nigel Cross had mentioned it to me, but nothing was proven. "How much did he supposedly owe?" I asked.

"Anywhere between two hundred grand and a million, depending on who you ask." I nodded but couldn't say anything. A million dollars in gambling debts was one heck of a losing streak.

"So what's this about someone else at the Westin?" Keller asked. His jaw was set and he glanced up at his partner. I smiled to myself and waited for Peters to place his hand on John's shoulder like a father forcing his stubborn child to do the right thing.

I pointed at the picture of Ben Davis on the top of the stack I'd handed to Keller. "That's the guy who went berserk and forfeited his game against Elena," I said. "He's also staying at the Westin where, of course, this all started."

"Just because he's staying in the same hotel and let off some steam under pressure doesn't mean he killed a guy," Keller said.

I looked up at Peters, and he shrugged. He'd backed me up already, so I was on my own.

"What?" Keller asked innocently.

"You actually accused me of murdering a friend because I happened to walk into the building that day, but a guy who really has motive, is obviously on edge and is staying in the same hotel as the victim doesn't even warrant questioning? Don't you see how blatantly absurd that is, John?"

"Don't get all high and mighty, Ray. As far as I'm concerned, you're still on the top of my list. No one who isn't involved finds two bodies in so short a time."

Obviously, our moment of congeniality was over. "You're right, John," I said, "I am involved! I'm trying to find out what happened to my friend. What are you doing? I just handed you sixty-three potential suspects, all of whom knew both victims and had motive."

I wasn't so sure if the US Chess Champion title and fifty thousand dollars was enticing enough to kill two people, but I was talking fast and Keller didn't ask.

"Maybe we would know more right now if you hadn't arrested me to make yourself look good," I yelled. "Maybe she would be alive and giving you answers because *I* would have been out doing *your* job!"

"This conversation is over," Keller said. "From now on, you keep your nose to yourself. You bring anymore dead bodies to my attention and I'll haul you in again, no questions asked."

"Maybe if you were working the case, *you'd* find them," I mumbled as he walked away.

"What's that, Ray?" he said. "Did you say something?"

"Nope. Must have been your imagination."

"Must have," he said with a scowl. He turned and stomped into Elena Johnson's room to bring misery to someone else.

"The Hardy Boys are better detectives," I said.

Mark Peters arched his eyebrows. I took that to mean he agreed.

22

☐ It was late but murder investigations never stick to a regular nine to five schedule. Since Detective Keller was sulking about his partner bringing in a suspect without his knowledge, he took a couple of uniformed cops to track down Ben Davis. I followed Detective Peters to the police station where Ryan Brooks was still waiting to finish up his interview.

Rows of florescent lights spread a hazy antiseptic glow over the mostly empty squad room. Abandoned desks and an occasional ringing phone in the back corner created a forlorn sense of something being terribly wrong, as if we'd stumbled upon a catastrophic event that had sent all the cops running.

Peters didn't seem to notice though, and I followed him to his desk where he shucked off his great long coat that could have been made into two, draped it over the back of his chair and then picked up a pink square of paper stuck to his computer screen. He glanced over the note and then set it on the desk. "Okay," he said, "he's been fed. Let's go see your chess guy."

We followed a maze of hallways with white-tiled floors and gray walls decorated with bulletin boards and doors identical to the bulletin boards and doors we'd just left in another hallway. I figured the building had been remodeled since I'd last been there because I was completely lost. Finally, Peters pointed me to a door while he went through the next one. A small placard above his door labeled the room as INTERROGATION 2. My door was blank.

The room I stepped into was about the size of a standard closet. There were two metal folding chairs the color of plastic model battleships facing a large window and the walls were painted flat black. It was an observation room. From my days as a cop, along with countless scenes from movies and TV cop shows, I knew the window was actually a two-way mirror. I could see into the interrogation room but whoever was in there saw only his reflection in a mirror. I dropped my coat on one of the chairs and stood with my arms folded.

The interrogation room I looked in on was a small square space with a basic table and two chairs. The walls, like everywhere else in the police station, were gray, the floor was covered with white vinyl tiles and there was a row of florescent lights on the ceiling. I watched as Detective Peters closed the door behind him and sat at the table with his back to me. Across from him was Ryan Brooks. On the table between them was an open pizza box with two slices of Hawaiian style inside.

"Sorry about that, Ryan," Peters said. His voice was tinny through a speaker mounted above the window, and

I glanced up to see a microphone hanging from the ceiling above the table in the interrogation room. "I didn't want to keep you waiting but I still have some questions for you. At least you got some dinner though, huh?"

Ryan nodded and sipped from a straw in a paper cup he brought up from his lap. "I need to get going though. I have a game tomorrow, and I haven't had any time to prepare."

"I'll be quick," Peters said. "Why don't you start by telling me why a really good chess player would resign against an inferior attack?" I'd given the detective two questions about Charlie's last chess game to ask without any preamble. Hopefully, Ryan wouldn't think too hard about them.

Ryan shrugged. "He wouldn't."

"Then why did Charlie resign against you the other night?"

"He didn't. We just never..." Ryan quit talking and slouched in his chair.

"Why don't we cut the bullshit now," Peters said.

"Do I need a lawyer?"

"Did you kill Charlie Roggenbuck?"

"No."

"Then you don't need a lawyer. How about you just tell me what happened."

"Who's in there?" Ryan asked with a nod toward the mirror. "How'd you know about the game?"

"Ray, you might as well come in here," Peters boomed as he raised his voice a bit.

I grabbed my coat and moved into INTERROGATION 2. "Hello, Ryan," I said as I closed the door behind me.

"Gordon. What's this all about?" he asked. "They arrest you and then drag me in for questioning? What's up?"

"I'm off the hook, Ryan. Something else has happened."

"What?"

I looked at Peters and he nodded. "Elena Johnson was shot and killed earlier tonight," I said.

Ryan's eyes went round, and he slumped back in his chair. "When? Who did it?"

"We don't know yet," Peters said. "Right now let's talk about the last time you saw Charlie Roggenbuck."

Ryan nodded. "All right. What do you want to know?"

"Were you playing a game of chess with Charlie Roggenbuck the night of his death?"

"Yes." Ryan's face was ashen, and he stared at the middle of the table.

"Why did you kill him?"

"I didn't. I told you that already."

"How'd he die?"

Ryan shrugged. "Looked to me like someone shot him."

"And how would you know that, Ryan?" Peters asked.

"I've seen movies," Ryan answered, then he quietly added, "but they never show it like that."

"So you were playing a game with Charlie Roggenbuck," Peters said, "then someone else came into the room and shot him, but you didn't see who. Is that right?"

Ryan shook his head. "No. Of course it's not right." He took a deep breath, which seemed to help raise him up from his slump and he put his elbows on the table. He drew another sip of soda from the straw and said, "Yes, I was playing a game with Roggenbuck. We were talking about you actually, Gordon. He even called you." Peters glanced at me, and I nodded to confirm what I'd already told them about Charlie inviting me to his hotel for a drink.

"Go on," Peters said to Ryan.

"Okay. So we were playing and after a while I ran out of chips. I told him I could use a break anyway so I went to get something else to eat."

"Where'd you go?" I asked.

"Across the street. There's a drugstore. I bought some peanuts, some chips and a Mountain Dew."

"Do you have the receipt?" Peters asked. Ryan screwed up his face as if to say that was the most absurd thing he'd ever heard. "We'll need to verify it," the detective added.

"Be my guest," Ryan said. "I'm sure they have security tapes or something."

"Then what happened?" I asked.

"I went back to the room."

"And?" Peters prompted.

Ryan shook his head and stared at the middle of the table again. The color in his face drained away, and the florescent lights gave him a greenish pallor that made him look both ghoulish and sick at once. "No," he said. "I don't want to."

Detective Peters put his elbows on the table and leaned forward. "Ryan, I know how difficult this is for you, but you have to tell us what you did, how things happened and what you saw. We have to know your side of the story in order to determine your innocence." He spoke slowly, and his voice was bottomless like a gentle grandfather trying to coax a scared little boy into telling the truth.

Ryan took another deep breath and sighed. It was a resignation to relive the horror of that night, but it also seemed to give him strength as he sat up straight. "The door was open a bit. I figured Charlie had left it that way so I wouldn't have to knock, so I just went in and..."

"And?" Peters said again.

"And he was dead! All right? He was kind of sitting on the floor next to the table. At first I thought he'd fallen down, so I kicked his foot and he fell over. Then I saw all the blood." Ryan covered his face with his hands. "Jesus, I can't get the image out of my mind."

"What did you do then?" Peters asked. "It's very important you tell us exactly what you did."

"What do you think I did? I freaked! I grabbed all my stuff and put it outside the door, then I wiped down everything I could remember touching."

"Why'd you do that, Ryan?" I asked.

"Are you kidding me? I watch TV," he said, and then he looked at Peters. "They call me 'Smudge.' I had to wipe my prints off the pieces, too."

"Why didn't you just call the police?" asked the detective.

Ryan shook his head. "I know I should have, but I would have been disqualified from the tournament. We're not supposed to play outside games with the other players. If they found out, I might have been banned for years."

There was no place for me to sit, so I was pacing the room behind Detective Peters. Ryan was hiding his face in his hands again, so Peters craned his neck to give me a quizzical look. "It's not viewed as study time when you play other opponents of the same tournament," I said. "Collusion would be very easy for a couple of grandmasters if they memorized a game together."

Peters nodded. "Okay. You wiped the chess pieces off because you left cheesy crumbs and fingerprints. Then what?"

"Wait a minute," I said. "Ryan, why did you knock over Charlie's king?"

Ryan frowned in confusion. "I didn't. I never touched his king."

I retrieved the picture of the chessboard I'd taken in Charlie's hotel room and showed it to Ryan. "Maybe you bumped the table?" I asked.

"No way. I even looked everything over before I left. That king was standing."

"So between the time you left the second time," Peters said to Ryan, "and when you got there," he looked at me, "someone else was in the room."

I nodded. Carla and I had arrived at the Westin Hotel about eight p.m. Ryan said he left at five thirty p.m. after coming back from the store, which gave someone else about two and a half hours to go in, tip over the King for whatever reason, and then leave without any sort of suspicion.

There was a knock, and the door opened. Detective John Keller stepped into the room and stopped when he saw me. "What in the hell is he doing in here?"

Peters stood up, towering over everyone, and said, "Well, I thought I could use a…"

"Forget it," Keller snapped. He then pointed at Ryan and said, "Let him go. You two, come with me."

John led Mark Peters and myself back to the face-to-face desks they called an office. They both sat down in their respective chairs while I leaned against a neighboring desk.

"So while you two have been wasting the department's resources on that walking bag of potato chips, I found something very interesting," John said.

When he didn't continue I said, "What, you need a drum roll? Come on, let's have it."

"Ben Davis is missing," he said triumphantly.

I looked at the suddenly silent Detective Peters and then back at John. "So? Are you saying we have a third victim?"

John shrugged. "Maybe, but I don't think so. He vacated his hotel room without checking out. Just left. He's gone, and before you say anything, Ray, airport security has already been notified and have his picture."

"What time did they realize he was gone?" Peters asked.

John laid a small notebook on his desk and flipped pages. He stopped and ran his finger down through his notes. "The cleaning lady went in at two thirty-six," he said.

"That was right after he blew up at the tournament," I said. I couldn't help but think if I hadn't been arrested,

Ben Davis would be in custody. Davis had almost nine hours to himself before Keller went in search of him. I shook my head but didn't say a word.

"Doesn't mean he left town though," John said. "I've got uniforms looking for him and we're checking other hotels as well."

"Did you talk to Nigel Cross?" I asked.

John shook his head. "No. Why would I?"

"If you want to know if Ben is still in the city, let's find out if he's still in the chess tournament."

23

☐ The clouds hung low the next morning. They blocked the view of Puget Sound but held the wind at bay. I consumed a plate-sized blueberry muffin and two strong cups of Starbucks house blend while I read the newspaper. For once John Keller had been right.

The story was in the lower right corner of the front page: "Checkmate is Murder for Two Championship Chess Players." The article described Charlie and Elena, both players in the US Chess Championship being held in Seattle. Neither player was a local and both were found dead in their respective hotel rooms—murder was suspected. While police weren't commenting, other resources said it was hard to believe the two killings weren't related.

As far as I was concerned, the media wasn't happy unless people were in misery, and there is nothing like a double homicide to write and talk about in order to scare the public. The television news was nothing more than a reality horror show, making the viewers nervous enough to keep watching and scary enough to make them tiptoe through their lives in fear of terrorists, plagues, another form of cancer or rampaging viruses—biological or digital.

The good news was Morphy would be coming home, but I couldn't pick him up until later in the morning. Instead, I picked up the phone and punched in Carla's number. "Are you alone?" I asked when she answered. "Shall I call back later?"

"Don't bother," she mumbled, "I'm making breakfast for one."

"Oh. Sorry," I said with a smile to myself.

"I'm not. It's okay, you know, if people don't spend the night after every date. It's actually kind of refreshing after all the crap we watch on TV."

"Have you seen the paper?" I asked.

"Not yet. Why?"

I filled her in on what had happened overnight and about Morphy. "He's going to be okay, though," I said. "He gets to come home today."

"Oh my God, Ray. Poor Morph. I saw that I missed a call from you last night. Is that why?"

"Yeah. I needed a shoulder to cry on."

"Oh, I'm so sorry."

"Don't worry about it. I had a murderer to think about anyway."

"That's not something to be kidding about, mister. You better be careful. Obviously someone out there has no problem with killing. Two dead bodies and a brick through your window…what's going on?"

"I don't know yet, but somebody thinks I'm getting close. They didn't throw anything at Keller anyway."

"What is it with you and John Keller?" she asked.

"What do you mean?"

"You've been angry ever since you saw him, and I don't think it's all about Charlie being killed either."

Carla was a woman who had a keen sense of things, especially when it came to me. She was part emotional barometer, part psychic. I nodded to myself. "I know," I said. "Old feelings, I guess. Unfinished business. Maybe I've been mad at him all these years without really knowing it, and then when I see him, boom."

"Yeah, boom is right. Maybe you should just let the past go, you know? Let him do his job." I knew she was right. Her levelheadedness was one of the things I loved about Carla, but I didn't say anything. "Be careful, Ray," she said.

"I will. Dinner later?"

"Sorry. I told you just because he didn't stay here or me there, it doesn't mean we had a lousy time last night."

"Right," I said. "Okay, I'll call you later and fill you in."

"You better."

I grabbed a jacket and headed for the Youth Center. Since Carla seemed to be doing okay with her date, I thought about going back to the Westin hotel and asking out Victoria. Maybe I would, but I thought what could be better than to play some chess, maybe even teach Alex a new opening, before bringing home my dog? At least it might keep my mind off of Carla and what she was doing with her artist boyfriend.

I checked in at the office of the Youth Center and told the receptionist I would be in the game room. There were two teenage girls standing in the doorway watching a boy of seventeen or so shoot pool. I excused my way through them, they giggled and then left.

"Have you seen Alex Donovan?" I asked the kid with the pool cue. He was about two inches taller than me and probably fifty pounds lighter. His clothes were baggy and faded, the jeans torn at the knees, the T-shirt frayed and thin. I wondered if they were old or given today's fashions, if he'd bought them like that new.

The boy frowned in confusion. "X," I said.

"Oh yeah, him. Nope." Our conversation over, he turned back to the pool table.

I took a seat by one of the chessboards and took out my cell phone. A digital voice found the number of the Hideout for me and then offered to connect me for an additional charge.

"Hideout," a human voice said after four rings.

"Hi. Is Tommy Ryder there by any chance?" I asked.

"Yeah. Wait one."

The line went silent, and I listened to the clacking of billiard balls and the whispers of the two girls who'd come back to stand in the doorway.

"Hello?" Tommy and I almost always spoke to each other in person when we're playing chess. Over the phone he sounded tired and academic.

"Tommy, this is Ray Gordon."

"Hey, hey! It's Ray! What're you doin' callin' me?"

"I was wondering if you'd heard anything is all."

"Well," he said, and his voice dropped to a conspiratorial whisper, "I heard about you getting arrested. I can hardly believe they did that."

"Well, you know who did it don't you?" I said.

"Yeah. Figures too. Don't know why there's so much bad blood between you two."

"He's the one with the problem, Tommy, and you know it." But I wondered about what Carla had said. Maybe I was harboring some ill will.

"Yeah, I know it. The way they talk around here, he's got a problem with everyone. My dad would probably knock him on his ass. He doesn't like it when one guy thinks his shit doesn't stink. Anyway, the problem from what I'm hearing, Ray, is you're the only one who's talking about the case."

"Maybe that's because it's Keller's," I said. "Are you going to be around for awhile?"

"Of course. Where do I have to go? Why?"

"I may need some help finding someone.

"Really?"

"And I might not. Don't know yet but I'll call you."

Mary Connor, Alex's counselor, came into the room and made a determined stride in my direction when she spotted me. I thanked Tommy and asked him to keep listening around, I'd call again.

"Hello, Mr. Gordon," Mary said. Her usual smile was strained under tight lips and concerned eyes.

"Hi, Mary. I came in to play some chess with Alex. Isn't he here today?"

She sat down and the smile flattened out. "Actually, we haven't seen him for a couple of days," she said. "I'm kind of worried, to tell you the truth. He's usually pretty good about letting me know if he's not going to be here."

We stood up together, and I made for the door. It wasn't unusual for some of the kids who frequented the youth center to not show up every day. Especially the teenagers who found other things to do with their friends—hopefully something that wouldn't get them in trouble. But Alex Donovan was a different story. Not only had he established a regular routine with punctual appearances, but he would actually call to let the counselors know when he wasn't going to show up. Part of his responsibility I proudly attributed to myself. Our chess lessons and games were ongoing, and I would purposely end our matches before we finished so Alex could write down the position, study it and return with a plan to finish it out.

Alex was a good kid. He always cleaned up after using the facilities of the youth center, he put away the chess pieces, and re-racked his cue after a pool game, he had stopped fights and helped younger kids find their way around the building. The counselors confirmed he'd never been in any legal trouble either. Which was saying something when talking about teenagers with little to no parental guidance in their lives. But it had taken him a while before he was comfortable.

Alex had shuffled into the Brookstone Youth Center one day, soggy and sniffling. He'd said "Hi" and then went into conversation lock down but allowed himself to be shown around. He graciously took a towel and dried off and then wandered about as if inspecting the place. Apparently, the center passed muster because he was soon coming in to shoot pool and play chess every Monday,

Wednesday, and Friday. After a while he stopped playing pool. When he started calling me "Gordo", the counselors told me it was a sign of trust.

I turned slowly onto Rosemont Street and swiveled my head back and forth to find a set of house numbers. I wanted evens so I concentrated on the left. When I found Alex's house, I understood why he chose to hang out at Brookstone three times a week. The front lawn was a mass of strangled brown grass, patches of trampled earth, and a brigade of dusty-green prickly weeds entrenched along the sidewalk. Scattered around the lawn were a jumble of faded plastic toys and a couple of askew metal and vinyl strollers that wouldn't pass safety inspection in any country.

I high-stepped my way to the front stairs where a rusty handhold made of old pipes wobbled like a freshly sprung jack-in-the-box when I grabbed it. The house itself was shaped like a giant shoebox with a pointy lid. It was layered with decayed pink adobe veined with cracks and scabs of gray where chunks of the surface had broken and fallen away. The windows were covered in plastic to help keep out the cold, and the house numbers I'd spotted from the road hung lazily above the door and were droopy with cobwebs.

I pressed an unadorned round button set into the wall next to the door and waited. After a few moments, I pounded on the door with my fist and turned back toward the street and watched an abandoned plastic bag drift between cars like a lonely dog.

When the door behind me finally opened, I spun around to face a woman who could have found work in Hollywood as a boulder. She was a foot shorter than myself and roughly the same shape as the Volkswagen Bug Charlie drove in college. Her expression was pinched, and even though she was short, she seemed to look down on me. Her paste colored pageboy hair hung with the weight of a missed wash—or three.

"Yeah?" she croaked around a cigarette glued between her thickly coated red lips. "What do you want?"

I took a half step backwards. "Are you Mrs. Donovan?"

"Mrs. Kilpatrick now."

"I'm sorry. I'm looking for Alex Donovan. I thought he lived here."

"Uh huh," Mrs. Kilpatrick said. "And who are you?"

"My name's Ray Gordon. I'm Alex's chess coach at the youth center." I held out my hand but let it drop when she just looked at it.

She opened the door wider and revealed a toddler straddling her wide hip. "I see," she said. "Well I'm his mother, and I haven't seen him yet today."

"So he's not home?"

"Didn't I just say that I haven't seen him today?"

"Actually you said 'yet.' I thought maybe he was still asleep in his room or something."

Her eyes rolled a bit as she shifted the kid, and she turned so her head disappeared behind the door. "Ronald have you seen Alex this morning?" she asked. No answer. "Ronald!"

I heard laser bursts or machine gun fire or both being blasted from a television speaker. I inched forward enough to chance a peek inside the house. A young man in his early twenties was sitting on the floor with his back against a sofa covered by a bed sheet. He wore thinning blue sweatpants and a white T-shirt. His face was pale and contrasted with a patchy black beard of four or five days' growth while his hair looked like a bird's nest that had been demolished by a mean kid with a pack of firecrackers.

"Ronald!" Mrs. Kilpatrick yelled again. The young man shook his head without removing his gaze from the TV in front of him, and I stepped back to my place on the porch.

"Ronald ain't seen him neither," Mrs. Kilpatrick said as she turned around. "We don't know where he is."

"Any ideas?" I pressed. "He hasn't been to the youth center for a few days. We just wanted to check up on him to make sure he was okay." Unlike you, his own mother, I thought.

She shrugged. "Don't know."

"How about his father?" I tried.

"Nope. Alex's dad is in Walla Walla. Has been for the past two years. Don't expect to see him back around here for another three or four. Understand?"

I understood. Walla Walla was home to the Washington State Penitentiary. "Well, if you see Alex will you let him know I was here and I'm looking for him?"

She nodded. "If you find him first send him home. He owes me money, and I'm outta smokes."

"Sure. I'll let him know." She shut the door, and I stepped back down into the yard. With his father in prison and his mother more concerned with her stash of cigarettes than her son, it really was no wonder why Alex preferred the youth center to his home life. Which is why I was even more worried than I was before about where he might be.

24

☐ Morphy's homecoming was like seeing a dear friend at a funeral. There were hugs and smiles shaded by regret and sorrow. We both knew something bad had happened and that it had somehow changed things between us. People who didn't have a dog might not understand, but there was emotion, a sense of guilt on my part for not preventing what had happened, and a feeling of sadness from Morphy, maybe for the same reason, maybe because he felt bad about not being able to go out and chase cats out of the yard. Regardless, I scratched his ears and rubbed his tummy, but I couldn't help shedding some guilty parental tears. Morphy's right shoulder was shaved bare all the way down to his paw so he looked like a quarter of him was shorn sheep. White bandages covered his stitches and were wrapped tightly with gauze, making him walk with a limp, and I envisioned him as "The Mummy's Pet." The worst insult though, was the plastic cone: sixteen inches in diameter, it was wrapped around Morphy's neck and designed to keep him from licking his wound but looked perfectly capable of receiving transmissions from space.

Morphy knew he looked foolish, and when I refused to remove the cone he skulked under the table and maneuvered himself down to the floor with a sorry look of dejection. I placed a bacon-flavored, cat-shaped chew toy I'd bought as a welcome home gift within his reach and picked up my phone. It was time to find Charlie Roggenbuck's mystery woman named Sara.

Deacon Kamalov at the St. Nicholas Russian Orthodox Church was glad I called because he'd been meaning to get in touch with me. Since I was in the Magnolia area and he was up on Capitol Hill, we decided to meet in the middle at Seattle Center, for lunch.

I made sure Morphy had a blanket, a handful of treats, and plenty of water. I told him I had to leave and to just rest, then at eleven I left to make sure I'd be on time to meet the Deacon. With the Key Arena, Pacific Science Center, the Space Needle, Experience Music Project, the carnival, and other activities at the Seattle Center, finding someplace to park wasn't a problem. Surrounding the area were a host of parking lots, each proud to display their daily and hourly rates like cheap motels.

I parked on 6th and paid the daily rate. I trotted across the street and skirted past the wavy lines and metallic colors of the ultra modern Experience Music Project, an interactive music museum featuring the relics of rock and roll legends and offering participants a venue for beating drums, singing and even taking the stage for a concert.

The carnival was open but barren and still in the chilly weather. Only the miniature golf course and bumper car ride, both indoors, showed signs of life.

I bowed under an icy gust and ducked into the food court where I had agreed to meet Deacon Kamalov. The building had a large open space ringed with vendors serving a variety of food. Some of the glaring neon signs were recognizable brands; Pizza Hut served it by the slice, Baskin Robbins offered their thirty-one flavors of ice cream even in January, and hamburgers and french fries were available at McDonalds. Then some regional and local restaurants offered everything from fresh fish to sub sandwiches, homemade fudge to oriental salad.

The middle of the food court was filled with a slew of tables and chairs, which were only in use during the winter months. Most people wanted to sit outside and enjoy their food while watching street entertainers. But it was January, and it was cold. The usually die-hard puppeteers, who danced their string-a-long friends for pocket change, were nowhere to be seen, and the tables in the Seattle Center Food Court were packed.

I bought a bag of candy corn at the Sweets Factory and wandered through the jumble of tables until I found an unoccupied seat. Deacon Kamalov spotted me just as I sat down and for all his roundness, deftly made his way to my table.

"Mr. Gordon," he said, "so nice to see you again."

"You too, Father. Would you like some candy corn?"

"Thank you," he said as he dipped his thick fingers into the bag.

"So what do you want to talk to me about?" I asked.

"Right to the point then, eh Mr. Gordon?"

"Call me Ray," I said with a smile. The more he talked, the more candy corn for me.

"All right then. Ray. The woman you came to me about? Sara? She wants to help you, but she is afraid."

"Wait a minute. You've talked to her again? Since you gave her the note from Druga?"

"Yes. She is grateful for your help, but she is scared."

"Of what?"

"What has already happened."

"She thinks she's involved somehow?" I asked. Kamalov nodded and fingered more candy. "Did she know Elena Johnson?"

He shrugged. "I don't know."

"Father, why are you here?" I asked. "You've told me nothing you couldn't have said over the phone."

He nodded and glanced at the people surrounding us. "You must understand she is very afraid," he said.

"She's here isn't she?" I asked. My gaze darted from face to face, searching for a woman I'd never seen.

"Yes. After reading this morning's paper, she called and insisted I introduce the two of you as soon as possible. And so, here we are."

"Yes. Here we are," I said. "But where is she?"

"I will get her," he said and pushed himself up and away from the cheap metal table. "I just ask that you remember she has lost a loved one."

"Of course," I said. So she *was* connected to Charlie.

He melted into the crowd, and within a minute his seat was taken. The woman who sat across from me was on the small end of five-six with shoulder length black hair and eyes the color of midnight. She sat lightly, like a nervous cat, hugging herself around a thick wool coat that brushed the ankles of her boots.

"Sara?" I asked. She nodded. "Do you have a last name?"

She nodded again but didn't say a word. Why did she want to meet me if she hadn't planned on speaking? I stared at her.

"But I will not tell it to you," she finally said.

"All right, your prerogative. Do you want to tell me why you wanted to meet me?"

"I understand you were a friend of my Charlie's?" Now it was my turn to nod. "And you're also an ex-police officer?" I nodded again and threw back a handful of candy corn. The chitchat was done, and the score was tied on questions answered silently.

"Do you think you know who killed him?" I asked. "Is that why you're here?"

"No. But I do know many people, mostly his chess friends, think he was a gambler."

"And you don't?" I said remembering Nigel Cross's surprise at hearing me mention Charlie's name in the same sentence as 'friend.'

"He never bet on anything. He didn't owe money to anyone like that."

"Okay. Did you and he have a son?"

She looked at the table then around at the people gorging themselves on high-caloric, greasy foods. Yum. Her eyes pooled with tears, and she blinked rapidly to keep them from rolling over. "Yes," she whispered.

"Why'd you tell Father Kamalov you didn't have a son?"

Her gaze fell to the table between us. "I didn't lie to him," she whispered. "I told him I was never a mother."

"I'm sorry about your loss."

"I'm sure that's none of your concern, Mr. Gordon," she said quickly. "If you're trying to find out what happened to Charlie, that's fine. Our son is no one's business. Period. Okay?"

"All right. I'm sorry." She picked at her fingernails, and I suffered through the silence with more candy. "Can I ask another personal question?" I said.

"I don't see how my personal life is of any relevance."

"Everything is relevant in a homicide investigation. As an outsider, any and all information is useful because I don't know what I'm looking for."

"Okay," she said quietly.

"Why didn't you and Charlie marry?"

Sara sat back in her chair and glanced around again as if making sure no one had heard her horrible secret. "I'm not sure how to answer that right now," she said. "I've told people different reasons, like he had to stay in New York and I had my life here, but that's not true." She pulled the collar of her coat tighter, and a tear finally broke the dam and trailed down her cheek. She looked at me apologetically and shook her head. I didn't try to stop her when she stood and walked away.

Sara was an enigma because she only wanted to help in a very limited way. If what she said about Charlie not gambling was true, then great. But I would have been able to come to that conclusion on my own without wasting any time.

It was what she wasn't telling me that I was interested in. With Charlie gone, she had nothing to lose or be embarrassed about in telling me the reason they never married. Would she have told the police in an official investigation? Did she not tell me because I wasn't official? Was she embarrassed? Was she hiding something?

I was positive the answer to more than one of my questions was 'yes' but Sara obviously had some pain just below the surface, something besides the loss of Charlie Roggenbuck. Maybe she was still afraid of her family. Whatever it was, she would have to brave it on her own before she would open up to me.

25

☐ And so I was starting with a clean plate. Charlie's murderer, who I presumed to be Ben Davis, though I didn't know what his motivation might be besides anger, had vanished. I'd decided against Elena Johnson being Charlie's reaper because she too was dead, but she'd known something or been wrapped up in whatever was going on. So I had nothing on that front. Charlie's "person of significance," Sara, had given me a little to nibble on though.

The information she presented was essentially useless, nothing more than an excuse to see me face to face. I had felt like an exhibit. She wanted to see me, size me up, and get a feel for my potential…threat? Ability to help? I wasn't sure. She certainly knew more than she let on, but I didn't think she was involved directly with the chess player murders.

The next thing I needed to do was find out why officials with the United States Chess Federation were so sure Charlie Roggenbuck had a gambling problem and why Sara was so determined to say otherwise. Gambling debts could easily be a motive for murder if Charlie was wrapped up with the wrong sorts. And it certainly wouldn't be something the USCF would like their star player being associated with. I was sure the USCF wouldn't employ mafia-style tactics and do away with someone they felt was a hindrance to their organization, but it would explain the upturned noses and undercutting remarks about Charlie. Sara, on the other hand, might have been in denial concerning her boyfriend's financial digressions or she simply didn't know about them. Or she was telling the truth.

I stepped out the west entrance of the food pavilion and walked across the plaza toward Key Arena where the Super Sonics used to play and rock bands played their versions of music. The Northwest Rooms, where the Chess Championship was being played, were in an L-shaped building hugging the northwest corner of Key Arena. I found Nigel Cross standing in the spot where I'd been arrested.

"Mr. Gordon," he said. "I see the police couldn't find a use for you."

"Not this time, anyway," I said. "Do you have a minute?"

"More questions? Or do you have some answers for me this time?"

"Questions, I'm afraid. But if they lead to answers, I promise to share."

"All right, Mr. Gordon. I'll take you up on that."

"What makes you so sure Charlie Roggenbuck had a problem with gambling?" I asked.

"Two reasons, actually," Nigel said. He motioned me to a bench along the windowed wall and sat down. "Not too long ago, Mr. Roggenbuck was on a winning streak. You may remember it, he won several international tournaments and came into a fairly large sum of cash from those winnings. Shortly thereafter, it was gone. I also know he frequented a casino out here in Washington."

"That's just speculation, Mr. Cross," I said. "Just because two separate events can be related doesn't mean they are."

"Are you familiar with Occam's Razor, Mr. Gordon?"

It sounded vaguely familiar, like the name of a song that hides while the tune dances tricks around the brain. I shook my head.

"Basically, it says that whenever you have competing theories about the same thing, the simplest is usually the correct one."

"Doesn't sound like a chess player's philosophy," I said. "Simplicity isn't how chess games are won." Usually.

"Touché. Nevertheless, Charlie had a way with money. He never seemed to hold on to his winnings. But I suppose that's a conversation you'd better have with his bank."

Nigel Cross stood and glanced at the clock, then his watch. "Charlie Roggenbuck was into something," he said. "Gambling or not. Like I told you before, a few years ago he changed. Whatever happened, it's too bad. He was a great chess player up to that point."

"His girlfriend had their baby while he was at a tournament in Europe, but it died," I said. "It's a good bet that's what made his mood change."

"I see. I'm sorry to hear about that. He never said anything."

"I've just heard about it myself. I guess it's not something he talked much about. I thought you should know, though, before the rumors about him get worse."

"I can appreciate that, Mr. Gordon. Thank you." Nigel gave his watch another look then gave me a nod that told me we were through and he walked away.

Charlie had been a good player up to that point, Cross said. Was it the death of his son? I didn't remember Charlie ever being anything less than a great chess player, but I wasn't ensconced in the chess world the way Nigel Cross was either.

I would have loved to go to New York and search Charlie's belongings and maybe even try to get into Elena Johnson's home. There might have been a wealth of information in written letters, emails, or notes of some sort. I was toying with the idea of calling Tony Druga again when Vladimir Penski caught my eye.

"Raymond," he said after I went into the playing hall and sat next to him, "you should go."

"Why?" I asked. "What's going on?"

"You are not welcome. People have been talking about you."

"Why? Come on, spit it out."

"You found both Charlie and Elena. They were our friends, our family, all of ours," he said, sweeping his hands over the room like a preacher on a pulpit. "The police think you killed them. They even arrested you for it! Now everyone here is wondering if it is true. They are scared and angry."

If John Keller knew what he'd done to my reputation, he'd be a three-toed sloth, lazing away the day with a shit-eating grin on his face. Making me look bad was probably his plan all along. I looked around the room and caught a few people staring. Even Ryan Brooks was glaring at me. I did notice that Ben Davis was missing though. He went berserk, yet I was the suspect. Nice.

"What about you, Vladimir?" I asked. "What do you think?"

He smiled, and I made a mental note to see my dentist for a check-up. "I know you wouldn't do this," he said. "Charles was your friend, but this doesn't make any sense."

"It makes sense to somebody. The trick is *finding* that somebody."

Vladimir nodded, but his eyes were focused elsewhere. I followed his gaze across the room where several of the players were gathered and looking our way. If they'd been dressed in jeans and leather jackets, hair slicked back and fidgety fingers curled into fists, I might have felt threatened, but sweaters and corduroys didn't have that effect. Nevertheless, their stares and under-the-breath grumblings made it clear that my presence wasn't wanted. Besides, one of these people had committed murder. Possibly twice.

"Maybe you should go now," Vladimir said.

26

☐ It was time for the next round of play to begin. Just as I decided it was indeed the moment for me to leave the tournament hall, Nigel Cross stepped up to the microphone at the head of the room and asked for everyone's attention.

"I regret to inform you..." he began. Everyone in the room groaned. Nigel held up his hands and regained some control. "Believe me people, I know how you feel. However, after the tragic loss of two of our friends, I feel this tournament must be cancelled."

The crowd burst into a cacophony of questions, boos, and confusion. I looked at the players, ready to tackle someone if he went for the director, but they were all still, arms folded or raised or jammed in their pockets.

Once things settled down again Nigel said, "I've discussed the situation with the USCF and frankly, we should have aborted the tournament after we lost Mr. Roggenbuck, but we thought things would even out. Now, with Miss Johnson's death, we feel it is prudent to stop play at this time. Are there any questions?"

The crowd erupted and pushed forward, which forced Nigel, once again, to demand silence. He then chose questions from the sea of upraised hands like a politician at a press conference.

No, there would be no US Chess Champion this year.

No monetary prizes would be awarded.

Yes, the simultaneous games with local schools would go on as scheduled, provided the players agreed to stay.

There were more questions from the players, mostly about costs and if they would be reimbursed for one thing or another. But at least there was some good news — the simuls. Simultaneous games were exhibition matches where a Grandmaster played any number of games, usually about twenty, at the same time. The boards would be arranged in a circular fashion with the opponents seated and playing the black pieces while the Grandmaster played white, strolled from one game to the next, made a move, and went on. The kids loved it because it might be their only opportunity to play a Grandmaster, and the schools loved it for the recognition as well as the encouragement for kids to play.

My concern though, was what Nigel Cross had said about players agreeing to stay. While Ben Davis's apparent lack of anger management skills and his sudden disappearance had me betting on him, if the killer turned out be another one of the tournament participants, the tournament itself was keeping the person in Seattle. Now with the remainder of games cancelled, there was no reason to stay and risk capture. The timetable to complete the investigation suddenly became much shorter.

"Where are you going?" Vladimir asked when I stood.

"I'm not going to let whoever did this get away with it," I said. "I'm going to go figure this out."

I pushed through the mob of chess players who clamored around Nigel and left the building, then crossed the plaza in front of Key Arena.

The wind had flared up to a squall, testing the tensile strength of several flags and banners as well as the thickness of my coat. No one else was braving the cold, and the closer I got to the food pavilion the more alone I felt.

But I wasn't alone. The hairs on the back of my neck came alive and put my senses on alert as a chill electrified my spine. I started to turn, but it was too late.

A hand smothered my mouth, and I felt a sharp, breathtaking agony plunge into my back. My legs gave out, the ground rushed up, and everything went black. I never saw a face.

27

☐ I mucked my way back to consciousness. It was a slow and blurry process, but I figured out I was in a hospital room and my right side felt like it had been whacked a few dozen times with a baseball bat.

"Oh good. You're awake," a woman's voice said.

I rotated my head enough to see the voice was attached to a nurse and was rewarded with a wave of nausea and a base drum thud on my brain. She was a little fuzzy and out of focus, but she left the room before I could ask if she was feeling all right. I sat up with a groan and looked around the room for my pants.

"You're a lucky man, Mr. Gordon," another voice said. This time it was a doctor, and the nurse standing next to him was now in focus.

"Really?" I asked. "Please tell me how this is lucky." I waved my hand at my bandage-encased torso. I looked like a campfire stick piercing a marshmallow.

"The blade you were stabbed with hit a rib which means you go home tomorrow sore as hell, instead of to the ICU with a pierced lung and hooked up to a machine for a few days."

"Lucky me."

"That's what I said."

When John Keller strolled into the room and flashed his badge, I was actually glad. Repartee with a witty doctor wasn't fun. Then John spoke, and my joy was blown out like a candle flame. "I hope this isn't some stunt," he said.

"Is your partner with you, John?" I asked.

"No. Why?"

"Because I don't want to talk with you. You have a very bad attitude, and you're mad because your investigation isn't going the way you want."

He rolled his eyes and turned to the doctor. "Doc? What's the story here?"

"Stab wound, detective. My guess would be with a small blade, maybe something like a Swiss Army knife, and a concussion. It looks like he hit his head on the concrete when his attacker let him drop."

"Is the stab wound self-inflicted?"

The doctor froze and squinted at Detective John Keller. Then his eyes popped open, and he shook his head like he was trying to rattle out the question. "Uh. No, detective," he finally said.

"You sure?" John asked.

"Detective," the doctor said, strained patience seeping into his voice, "the human arm cannot bend in such a way to stab oneself like that. Mr. Gordon is actually quite lucky."

"Why would you even ask something like that?" I asked.

John shrugged. "It's amazing what a scumbag will do to get the heat off."

"I thought I was off of your long list of suspects."

John shrugged again.

"I assure you Detective, Mr. Gordon's wound was not self-inflicted," the doctor said.

John nodded, though I couldn't tell if he was satisfied with the answer or just letting it go for the moment.

"Did you find Davis?" I asked.

"I'll fill you in later." Keller walked out into the hall and turned around. "I'll be in touch."

"Looking forward to it," I said. "Oh, and thanks for the get well card. It was touching."

The doctor stifled a laugh. and John frowned as he turned and stalked down the hall.

"You two don't get along, do you?" asked the doctor.

"You're a better detective than he is," I said with a nod toward the door. "What time is it anyway?"

"Almost ten."

I'd been out of it for hours. I had work to do and a dog to take care of. "Does this hospital have a records department?" I asked.

"What are you looking for?"

"Not a what, a who. I need the last name of a woman who had a baby a few years ago."

"Lots of women had babies, Mr. Gordon. And not all of them at this hospital."

"I need to start somewhere," I said.

"King County's public records are computerized. Make it easy on yourself, and go to the courthouse once instead of every hospital in town. It'll be quick, but not painless." When I gave him a look of not understanding he said, "County employees. You know."

"You do standup on open-mic nights don't you," I said with a smile.

"If only the nurses thought I was funny," he said and moved to the door.

"Well, good luck with that."

"I'll be back to check on you later. We'll get you out of here first thing in the morning."

"Thanks, Doc," I said.

Once the doctor was gone, I prodded my side gingerly. Like a knight on a center square of the board, able to attack all around, the pain rippled outwardly from the spot I touched until my entire side throbbed and my head beat an aggressive rhythm. I bit my lip and squeezed my toes together so I wouldn't make any noise. Once the pain ebbed, I was able to use my fingertips to maneuver the phone to where I could grab it off the bedside table and called Carla.

"Ray! Where have you been?" she mothered. "I thought you were going to call later, not *later*. You can't tell me you'll call and then not let me hear from you for so long while you're looking for a murderer."

"Well, that's kind of why I'm calling."

"What? What is that supposed to mean? What are you saying?"

"Carla, take a breath. I'm okay. I am in the hospital though." I filled her in on the day, Morphy being home alone, the woman I'd met at the Seattle Center, and the attack that landed me in the hospital.

"Oh my God, Ray. This is getting out of control," she said. "I wish you'd let it go."

"You know I can't do that," I said.

"I suppose not. I hope Charlie knows what you're trying to do for him."

"Do you think he would help if he could?"

"He'd probably try and turn it into a chess problem," Carla mused. "He's probably trying to figure out how to counter the offense as we speak."

"As long as he's got a pizza while he's doing it," I said with a smile.

"How can I help? Do you want me to go over and take care of Morphy?"

"No, that's okay. I'm kind of worried about him and Kortnie's closer."

"Ah, Kort-nie," Carla sing-songed. "You know she has a huge crush on you, and you're kind of leading her on by letting her take care of Morph all the time."

"I know she does, and I don't mean to, but she is closer."

"Are you telling me you wouldn't jump in the sack with her if she just came out and asked?"

I was pretty sure Carla was just having fun with me, but I thought I detected a hint of, not jealousy, but concern in her tone. "She's a looker," I said, "and she's nice, but mentally she's too messed up. Everything is a soap opera to her. No thanks."

"Okay," she said, and I could hear the smile in her voice. "Just so you know what you're doing."

"Carla…"

"Yes?"

"I've been thinking, especially lately…" I hesitated. I'd had too many painkillers for this particular conversation.

"What have you been thinking about, Ray?" she asked.

I took a deep breath. "Uh…I want to talk to you, but my head needs to be clear."

"Okay. I'm always here. You know that."

"I know."

"Call me when you're ready, Ray."

"I will," I said. "Thank you."

Kortnie was the one person in my immediate vicinity I could count on when it came to Morphy. Neighbors were fine for simple tasks like filling the food dish, but in a wounded state, Morphy needed extra attention. After all, this girl picked up his crap. We'd met while Morphy and I were out for a walk and she was moving into a rental with three other young women. Kortnie fell in love with Morphy instantly. The next time we ran into each other, at the grocery store, she asked how Morph was doing and offered to walk him for me. She didn't ask for money but told me she was studying veterinary science, and I put two and two together; student offering to work equals said student in need of cash. It worked out though, at least until her emotions started pouring out on my shoulder on regular occasions, but by then I was stuck.

Kortnie answered her cell phone on the fourth ring, and I gave her the good news/bad news routine. The good news was she would get to see Morphy; the bad news was that we were both hurt, which is why I needed her to go and take care of him.

"Oh my God!" she said. "What happened?"

I told her about the brick and Morphy getting cut but said it looked like something random so she wouldn't panic. "Probably just a couple of punks who got the wrong house," I mused.

"Okay," she said. "Poor Morph. And what about you? Where are you?"

"I'm at the hospital." Oops.

"What? Why? Are you okay? What happened? What's wrong?"

"Uh. Well. I was mugged. Got stabbed."

"What? Oh my God!" Then she was gone, the connection broken. I decided she must have fainted. Kortnie was definitely not as in control as Carla.

Less than five minutes later, I was debating on calling Kortnie again, wondering if something had happened when she burst into my room.

"Kortnie! Where were you when I called?" I asked. Whatever pain medication they had given me couldn't have been so strong I missed an hour between our phone call and her arrival. At least I hoped not.

"You could say I was in the neighborhood," she said and stepped closer. The left side of her face looked like someone had tried to mold a rotten eggplant to her cheek. The bruising was like a nebula, pink and red on the outer edge, purple in the middle and radiating out from her swollen watery eye.

Ignoring my own pain, I pushed myself into a sitting position. "Kortnie, what the hell happened to you?"

"Don't worry about me! You're the one who was stabbed!"

"Right. I told you what happened to me. Come on. What's going on here?" It had to have been her boyfriend,

Derek somebody. She was always crying about how he treated her. "Let me guess," I said. "Derek?" She sank into the chair beside my bed and stared at her toes. She nodded. "Did you call the police?"

She sniffled and shook her head. "Oh, I couldn't do that," she whispered.

I was an ex-cop, not really prone to violence, but idiots who punched women made me want to take the safety off my gun. Kortnie was a doe-eyed hottie who, while not completely emotionally stable, fawned all over this Derek guy she called a boyfriend, and he treated her like a stuffed toy.

"What's his name?" I asked.

"You don't need to worry about me, Ray. Look at you! And Morphy's hurt, too!"

"Kortnie, this guy is scum. He's no good for you. Come on, you can do a lot better than him, and you know it. Now what's his name?"

"You know his name. I've told you."

"Kortnie," I said, trying to reign in my anger. Not only was I mad at the guy who hit her, but at her as well for trying to protect him. Besides, it hurt the hole in my back to make an effort at volume. "I know his name is Derek. What's his last name?"

She stared at her toes and picked at her fingernails. I studied her and wondered what could possibly be going through her mind. Why would she want to protect someone who hit her? Kortnie sniffled, then nodded, as if coming to an agreement with herself. When she looked at me, her cheeks were smeared with tears.

"Griffith," she said. Then she stood up. "Can I get you anything? Do you hurt?" And just like that any thought of Derek Griffith vanished.

"No. I'm all right," I said. "The doctor said I can go home tomorrow. But Morphy hasn't had anything to eat for a while and he's recovering. But you need your rest, too. I'll call someone else."

"No, no," she said, "I'm on my way home. I would love to see Morphy. He always makes me feel better."

As much as I wanted Morphy to be spoiled, the idea of Kortnie alone in my house with someone throwing bricks through the windows wasn't appealing. "Why don't you just take him home with you?" I said.

"Maybe I will," she said. She leaned over the bed and kissed me on the cheek, soft like a friend, but with enough pressure to make me think about it. "See you tomorrow then," she said.

28

☐ Something Nigel Cross had said to me the day before came back to visit during the night, and I woke up with an idea about the correspondence game I was playing with Simon Waller. From memory, I sketched the board and position of the pieces on a slip of hospital stationery and recalled my initial analysis from when I was at the church.

Both Kings were under attack, though neither was in check, and it was my move. Nigel had mentioned Occam's Razor, a theorem touting simplicity or the obvious. Simon had moved his pawn to g4, which, after I'd had time to think about it, was a mistake. I worried about the black Queen moving to h3 to put my King in check and then the black Rook would slide over to the h-file to protect its Queen while she delivered mate. The simplest way for me to avoid that situation was to do the same thing to my opponent.

BLACK

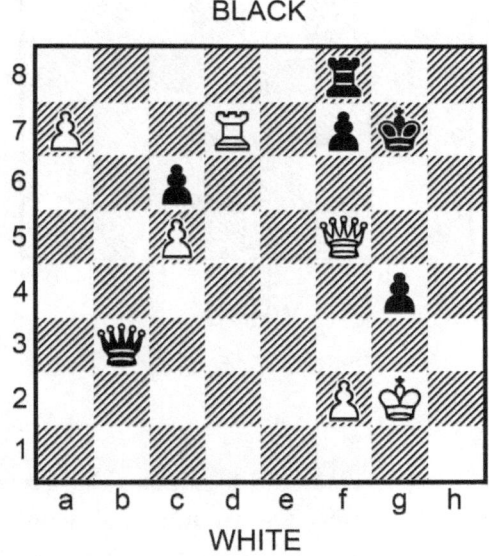

Position after 44. ...g4

If I captured the g4 pawn with my Queen and placed Simon's King in check, he would be forced to move the King to f6, h6, h7 or h8.

BLACK

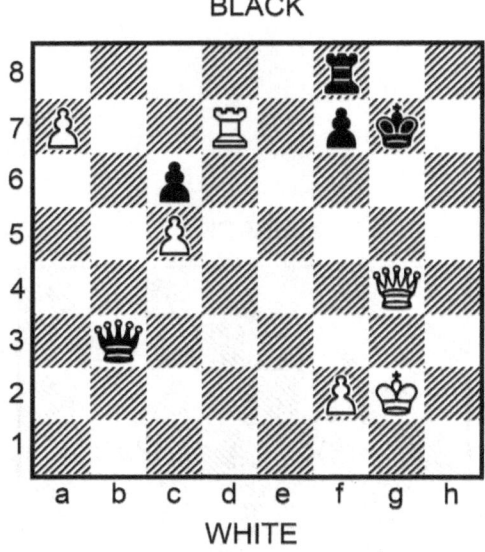

WHITE

Position if 45. Qxg4+

If the King went to the f6 square, the game would soon be over. Either my Queen and Rook would deliver checkmate, or he would lose his Queen to my Rook. If Simon placed his King on the h-file, I planned to bring my Rook to the d1 square in preparation to slide it over to the h-file and mate his King there. The beauty was that by capturing Simon's g4 pawn with my Queen, the d1 to g4 diagonal was under her influence. My Rook on the d1 square would be protected, and Simon would either have to exchange his Queen for my Rook or lose the game.

I smiled while I wrote out the analysis and hoped it was accurate and not a drug-induced hallucination brought on by painkillers and a need for something good to happen in a hellish week.

After a breakfast of bland scrambled eggs, cardboard toast, and a plastic cup of orange juice, Dr. Clark arrived and released me from the hospital as promised. Within moments, Detective Keller strolled into my room and demanded an interview before I left the hospital.

"What, exactly, do you want, John?" I asked, as I buttoned up my shirt. It still had a hole in the back, but had been cleaned. I'd had a lot of time to think during the night and besides having a revelation about the correspondence chess game, I made two decisions. One, it was time I made Carla a real part of my life and two; I needed to stop acting like a child when it came to Detective John Keller.

"I want you to tell me what happened yesterday," he said.

"I don't remember a whole lot. I was stabbed."

He paused and looked at me as if he sensed my change in attitude but didn't know what to make of it. "Did you see your attacker? Hear anything or smell anything significant? Come on, you know the drill," he said.

"I'm sure it was a man," I said. "Strong hands. He clamped my mouth shut and held my head so I couldn't look back. Next thing I know, I'm in here."

"Think it was the same person who killed Roggenbuck and the woman?"

"I don't know. Probably. It makes sense. What about Ben Davis? Did you find him?"

Keller shook his head. "Not yet, but that guy you mentioned the other night." He flipped a page in his notebook and slid his finger down the paper. "Nigel Cross said he forfeited."

"What do you mean? He dropped out of the tournament?"

"That's what I mean. He dropped out and disappeared."

I looked out the window and scanned the city. Buildings popped up behind trees and reflected the leaden sky back at me from their windows like dead eyes. What was going on?

"Was Davis a real player?" Keller said.

"Of course," I said turning around.

"So you know him?"

"No, I don't *know* him. Not like I knew Charlie, but I've played him before. Ben's a good chess player."

"Would he kill two people and then try to kill you over a chess tournament?"

I shook my head. "People do stupid things, John. Remember the lady who hired someone to kill the girl who took her daughter's spot on the cheerleading squad? As for why I'm not dead, I don't know. I should be. Maybe he didn't have enough time, or he was worried about the players leaving and seeing him."

John nodded and stared out the window. "MO's different though, knife instead of a gun. Couldn't risk the shot being heard maybe. And then there's the gambling angle," he said.

"And then there's the gambling angle," I repeated, but my heart wasn't in it. I could have been wrong, but it just didn't make sense. Charlie wouldn't gamble on chess games. Or would he? Did the death of his son change him so much? Tony Druga *had* told me about the casino manager he knew Charlie was looking for. Would it be a mistake to not tell John Keller about him? "Anything else I can do for you, Detective?" I inquired.

"Where are you going?" he asked, his eyes blinking up at me.

"Shopping," I said, wiggling a finger through the bloody hole in the back of my coat.

John nodded. "Be careful," he said and left.

I picked up my phone and called Tommy Ryder. I filled him in on what happened and said, "So I could use some help."

"Absolutely," he said, "but next game I get Knight odds whether you're in the hospital or not. Deal?"

Knight odds meant I would have to start the chess game with one of my Knights already removed from the board. "Deal," I said.

"Okay then, what do you need?"

"I'm looking for a guy named Sam Scott. He works in a casino somewhere in Washington State."

"A casino somewhere in the state," Tommy said. "Shouldn't be too hard."

"Start with the ones closest to Seattle."

"Has this got something to do with the chess player murders?"

"It might. There are some rumors that Charlie owed money and was looking for this guy. There might be a connection or maybe it's nothing."

"So what do you want me to do when I find him?"

"Give me a call and tell me where he is."

"That's it?" Tommy asked. He sounded like I'd just ripped him off.

"That's it," I said and smiled. "I just want to talk to him."

I took a cab from the hospital back to the parking lot where I'd left my car. Keller hadn't offered me a ride, but I doubt if I would have accepted if he had, and I didn't want to keep pestering Carla.

Since the time my car had been in the parking slot exceeded the amount of time I'd paid for, not only did I have to shell out enough cash for the extra time, but also a "small processing fee." A processing fee for a parking lot! What, exactly, needed to be processed?

Once behind the wheel, I tested the feel of the seat against my back. I'd never been stabbed before so I wasn't sure what it was supposed to feel like. It hurt. My entire back was a world record charley horse, tight and unyielding. I drove out of the lot hugging the steering wheel and with my butt hanging off the front edge of the seat. The parking lot attendant watched me leave, but I ignored him. I knew I looked like a scared old lady.

Traffic wasn't too bad, and I eased the Land Cruiser east along Denny Way. At 5th Avenue, I took a right, cruised beneath the two-way tracks of the monorail, and then pulled into another parking lot across the street from the Westin Hotel and Westlake Center.

Whoever attacked me had also ruined a perfectly good leather jacket. Not only was there a gash in the back but I'd leaked enough blood to make repair and cleaning a moot point. So I needed a new coat.

Shopping wasn't the most exciting thing to do on my list but I'd picked a location where I could find something and be on my way home within the hour. To my left was Nordstrom, an entire block of real estate with several floors dedicated to men's fashion; to my right was Macy's, another retail giant with its own block of territory and directly in front of me was Westlake Center, a mall stuffed with a variety of clothing chains.

At times, I thought I really needed a woman in my life.

Morphy was glad to see me when I got home. He wagged his tail with such force it sent the plastic cone around his head swinging in the other direction, making him look like a giant bobble-head toy. He hobbled to greet me, and it was an effort for me to keep from bawling with both parental joy and guilt.

On the kitchen counter next to the jar of dog biscuits was a bright red envelope with my name printed on the front. I tore it open and wasn't surprised to see that it was a get well card from Kortnie. The sentiment was nice, and I instantly wondered if I should go out and get her a card wishing her well in her own recovery. It was her handwritten note that stopped me.

> *Ray –*
> *You're the best! I really really hope you're*
> *feeling better because I want to thank you*
> *for everything you've done for me!*
> *Actually paying me to walk Morphy is over*
> *the top! Get better soon!*
> *P.S. I didn't want to go home alone so I*
> *slept in your bed. Hope you don't mind!*
> *Love Kortnie!*

I sat down at the kitchen table to think. A) I had enough trouble going on right now. B) Look at all those exclamation points! C) She slept in my bed?

I looked at Morphy for help, but he just sat on his haunches and swept an arc across the floor with his tail. I pushed myself up from the table, gave him a handful of dog treats, and went out to check the mail.

While there was nothing interesting in the mailbox, a note had been taped to my front door. It was a sheet of ordinary unlined paper, folded into fourths, with my name, *Raymond Gordon*, printed in block letters. I dropped the junk mail onto a small table just inside the door and gingerly unfolded the note touching only the corners. In the same block lettering it read: *Leave it alone. It's all over now.* I opened the door again and glanced up and down the street but the note could have been there for days. My garage was attached to the house, and I didn't normally look at the front door when I drove in. I'd usually stop at the head of the driveway and pick up the mail before coming in, and when I went out to get the paper each morning I'd be lucky to notice if I had pants on first.

I went back inside and sat at the kitchen table again. I flattened the note out in front of me using two butter knives to hold the ends down. I hoped there would be fingerprints, and Keller would be able to quickly put an end to the investigation.

By leaving the note, my opponent was requesting a draw. The problem I saw, however, was my opponent had already accomplished what he'd set out to do. Charlie Roggenbuck was dead, Elena Johnson—who was involved somehow—had been murdered, and I'd been attacked.

I'd played aggressive types before in chess tournaments. They would move a few of their pieces out and attack quickly, sometimes gaining space, sometimes winning material. Then I'd cautiously maneuver my pieces and advance slowly, constricting their movement while opening possibilities for myself. They would see their plan falter slightly and offer a draw before I could win.

Charlie Roggenbuck always said, "no one ever won by resigning." In this case, I felt the same about accepting a draw. My next move would have to be planned very carefully. If it was wrong, it could cost me the game, and this was one game I did not want to lose.

Morphy whined and looked at me seriously. I was sure Kortnie had taken him outside to attend to his business, but I wasn't sure what time she'd left. The cone that kept him from licking his wounds was too big to fit through the doggy door, so the note in front of me would have to wait.

"Come on, Morph," I said and pushed myself up. "Let's get some fresh air."

The pair of us limped and swayed into the backyard like a couple of aging hunchbacks with severe arthritis. Then we just stood there. It was cold, we were wounded, and since Morphy just stood next to me as if I was the one who needed to do something, I decided we'd been outside long enough.

When we turned to head back inside I was greeted by another note, this one spray-painted across the width of the back of my house. I was certain Kortnie hadn't left this one as her penmanship had more loops. It was a single word, graphically vivid in blood red enamel. Murderer, it read.

Three notes presumably left by three different people and only one an admirer. Lucky me.

29

☐ The King County Courthouse was a fat U-shaped block of concrete with the open end facing south. Its ten stories were stamped out at regular intervals with unimaginative windows, and it sat stoically on 4th Avenue as if refusing to give in to modern architecture.

Built in the early twentieth century, the courthouse looked like it would be more comfortable as a backdrop in an old black and white gangster movie than lumbering below the steel and glass giants of modern Seattle. It was often wrapped in scaffolding for renovations but continued its day-to-day county business.

Since I didn't need to be there at any specific time to do a search of birth records, I cruised down Elliott Avenue past the Youth Center and then south on Alaskan Way to look for Alex. I went by the aquarium and the arcade, the restaurants and the gift shops. There were plenty of kids, many Alex's age, but no Alex. I slowed to a crawl so I could stare at the lines of cars, bicyclists and pedestrians waiting to board the ferries bound for Bainbridge and Whidbey Islands. People spent the time waiting for their rides by reading books or newspapers and playing games. Some simply stared back at me.

None of them were Alex.

I turned east and eased by Safeco Field where the Mariners played and Qwest Field where the Seahawks rumbled, then took a left on 4th Avenue and looked for someplace to park.

The courthouse wasn't as uninviting as most county government buildings I'd seen. Maybe it was the grandfatherly look of the building itself, with its sandpapery feel, the grandiose moldings, and turn of the century finials. A small park filled with tall trees and littered with the homeless during warm weekends spread out in front of the south side of the courthouse. But I was certain the feeling of congeniality had something to do with the addition of computers. The less contact county employees had with the public, the more apt they were to be cooperative. At least that's what Carla had told me. She could have been kidding, but the dreamy yet dark look of a Monday morning in her eye at the time made me think it wasn't a joke.

Charlie's cousin, Tony Druga, told me Sara's baby was born four years after Charlie had returned to New York after graduating from the University of Washington in Seattle. I did the math in my head and wrote down the year the child was born, as well as the previous and following years for good measure. Then I wrote Sara's first name and the sex of her baby. I omitted the father's name because if she'd left him before the baby was born, I doubted his name would be on the official record. Better to get a thousand hits with the name Sara than zero success with Charlie Roggenbuck.

I handed the information card and the 'small processing fee'—another fee for no work I noted—to a burly, tight-haired, tight-lipped woman behind the counter. The simple action of retrieving my wallet sent jolts of pain like an electrical current from my slowly healing puncture wound up and down my back and legs. I winced and involuntarily jerked sideways like a marionette puppet with a bad string. The woman behind the counter looked at me blankly as if she saw similar behavior on a daily basis.

She glanced at the paper and pushed it back to me. "Wrong department," she said.

We stared at one another for a full minute before I raised my eyebrows at her. "And?" I asked.

"And what?" she fired back. "You're in the wrong place."

"Okay. Perhaps that 'processing fee' might buy me directions to the correct department?"

She stared some more and finally sighed. The only way to make a pest like me go away was to give me what I wanted. "You want the Administration Building," she said.

"Which is where?" I asked. I knew where it was, but I was amazed by her behavior.

The woman rolled her eyes and sighed. She shook her head slowly and pointed to her left. "One block up."

I smiled. "Whew! So much effort. Thank you. You've been *so* kind."

Across from the King County Courthouse on 4th Avenue was the King County Administration Building. Its architectural style is what I call "Nineteen Seventies Civic," built with glassy brown granite and capable of containing those voted into public office.

I'd been in the Administration Building several times but it was to get Morphy's dog license. I had no idea it was also where I needed to be in order to obtain birth records.

"Dog license time again?" I heard from behind me. I was a step away from the Vital Statistics office. I turned around and there was Carla Caplicki in a charcoal pant suit and a white blouse finished with a plastic ID badge dangling from her waist, looking every bit the public servant she'd always wanted to be. Her dark hair was pulled into a ponytail, and she held a clipboard against her chest with a pen entwined amongst her fingers.

"Hey there," I smiled and actually caught my breath.

"You're still alive, I see," she said.

"Honestly?" I said. "I don't really feel like it. Never been stabbed before. It hurts like hell, and I have a headache the size of Mt. Rushmore." She smiled. "Did I just ruin some big manly mental image you had of me?"

"Nope."

"Do you even have a manly mental image of me?"

"Now there's a question," she said. "How's Morphy?"

"He's doing okay. He doesn't like the big cone they strapped around his head, but it's better than not having him around at all." She pouted her lips at that. "I could use some help, Carla."

"Yeah? Personal? Professional? What?"

I handed her the information card I'd filled out over at the courthouse. "I'm trying to find Charlie's girlfriend, Sara, the one I told you about. They had a baby boy together, but all I know is her first name and about when he was born."

She put the card against her clipboard and looked it over. "Ray," she whispered, "you're asking an awful lot. There are reasons the county requires specific information. They're not going to just give you a list of women and their babies."

"I was hoping my ex-cop status would help," I said.

"It won't."

"Carla, I need to find this woman. If you have any ideas, I'm open to suggestions."

She glanced around the hallway, at the people walking by us, at the county employees darting in and out of doors. "I'm starving," she said. "Will you be a peach and get me a shrimp salad?"

"Be a peach? Who says that?"

"I do!"

"Okay, a shrimp salad. From where?"

"Wherever. But not fast food. Meet me in the upper south courtyard in a half hour. Okay?"

I nodded and Carla turned on her heel and marched down the hall.

Even in January, Seattle usually got very little snow, but it was still cold. I walked the three blocks to Mickey's Steakhouse slowly, avoiding any icy patches. The last thing I needed was to land on my ass and pop my stitches because I wasn't careful.

Mickey's Steakhouse was one of Seattle's great secrets. It was one of those places that didn't advertise and yet was always busy. The inside was intimately dark with dim overhead lights and a candle on each table. The menu changed daily and the waitresses looked like they just came from a law review. Above the door on the outside was a small brass plaque with the name *Mickey's* stamped into it.

I ordered two shrimp salads to go and was asked to have a seat. Mickey's isn't a "to go" sort of establishment but they do what they must to keep their customers happy.

On the way back to my rendezvous with Carla, I stopped in a mini-mart and bought two bottles of iced tea. It was thirty degrees outside and hot coffee would have been more prudent, but not with seafood. Not even with just shrimp salad. Coffee and seafood from Mickey's? I would have been run out of the city.

Carla was sitting on a concrete bench wrapped in what looked like a black sleeping bag with arms. The fur-trimmed hood encased her head, and the only way I knew it was her was because she waved me over.

I sat next to her and handed her an iced tea and the sack with the salads.

"Ooh. Mickey's," she said. "Why Mr. Gordon, I didn't know you cared."

"Oh, is that you in there, Carla?" I said peering into the hood. "You look like a periscope you know."

She slapped my shoulder, and I muffled a cry as the jolt rippled through my wound. "It's freezing!" she said. People in Seattle think forty degrees is freezing. She pulled her knitted maroon mittens off and deftly slipped a manila folder into the sack while reaching for a carton of shrimp salad. She put the sack on the ground and then with her booted foot, slid the package in front of me.

"How very secret agent of you," I said, retrieving my own salad.

"Just eat your shrimp, bub. I could lose my job over that. You owe me."

"I thought that's what the salad was for."

"Nope. I was just hungry."

"But it's from Mickey's!"

"True. I'll consider it a down payment. It's too cold out here, though," she said and stood up. "You can't properly enjoy a Mickey's shrimp salad when the shrimp are turning into ice cubes."

"Thanks, Carla," I said, standing up next to her. "Really."

"No problem. I hope it helps. Just burn it when you find what you need."

"Understood," I said and gave her a curt salute.

"And quit coming to see me at work only when you need help." Carla about-faced and shuffled back into the depths of the King County Administration Building. I wasn't sure, but I thought I could probably take that as an invitation of sorts.

Carla was right; it was too cold to properly enjoy a Mickey's shrimp salad. But I suffered through it, finished my salad, and when my rump was numb, I walked a block towards the parking lot where I'd left my car and sat down again at a bus stop to see what Carla had left in the sack. I was rewarded with twenty-three pages of paper bearing the information of all the women whose first name was Sara and who had baby boys over the specified three-year period. It even included their address at the time of the child's birth.

Sara P. Roggenbuck was the sixty-seventh name on the list. She'd named her son Gregory.

For all I knew, the name Roggenbuck was as common as Gordon, but I only saw the one. Tony Druga had made it clear—as did Sara herself—that Charlie was not married. Still, it made perfect sense for me to start my search with Sara P. Roggenbuck, even if she was number sixty-seven on the list.

I stuffed the pages back into the sack and headed down the street, glad I finally had something to go with. When I got back to my car, though, it wouldn't have mattered who on the list I'd decided to start with. I wasn't going anywhere for a while.

I'd parked in an unattended lot about two blocks from the courthouse. Five bucks for a few hours wasn't bad, even though I knew I'd only use a fraction of the time. But with an unmanned parking lot came risks—even in the middle of the day. My tires had been slashed.

It wasn't a random act either. All four of my tires were flat, and the cars on either side of mine were unmolested. Someone was upset with me, or they didn't want me to go anywhere soon. I looked around, hoping to catch the vandal enjoying his handiwork. The only person I saw looking in my direction was an old woman a block away, hardly the type to go around puncturing tires. It had to be the same person who'd tossed the brick through my window, which meant not only did the culprit know where I lived, he also knew what I drove.

I called a tow truck and mentally sifted through the names of possible suspects while I waited. Which of the chess players knew where I lived? I could have been followed home from the Seattle Center, but why go to all the trouble? If it was the same person who'd murdered Charlie, why not just kill me, too?

By the time I found the address given for Sara Roggenbuck by the King County records department, I had a new set of tires and swollen clouds had been unleashing torrents of rain for several hours. The sky had turned a thick, woolly black after the sun had set. Luckily the tow truck had arrived and secured my Land Cruiser before the rain started.

I parked in front of the house next door and killed the engine. Just as I was checking the address again, my phone chirped. It was Tommy. "Do you have some news for me?" I asked. Even though it was raining steadily and I was inside a car and about twenty-five yards away from the house, I kept my voice low.

"Your boy manages the Eagle's Nest Casino down by Olympia. You know where it's at?"

"Yeah, I've seen it. What is that racket? Where are you?" It sounded like he was calling from the middle of a children's TV show.

"I'm here, man," he said. "I looked the place up online, and I thought it sounded fun so I drove down. Spooked your boy though, I think."

"What do you mean you 'spooked' him? What did you do?" I kept my eyes on the house in front of me but so far all was quiet.

"I asked who the manager of the place was and they brought him over to me. I said I didn't want to talk to him, I just wanted to know who he was in case I won big and needed his assistance. He's been eyeing me all night now."

"Why'd you do that?"

"I wanted to check him out is all."

"Tommy," I said and shook my head, "rumor has it he's got ties to the mob back east. You might want to head home before you lose more than your shorts. I gotta go. Thanks."

The front door of Sara P. Roggenbuck's house had burst open. Voices spilled out but were lost in the pinging rain on the roof of my car. I could tell the person being pushed out the door was a man, but again, the rain spotting my windshield turned him into an abstract moving shape within a dark watercolor, and I couldn't make out any recognizable features. The accents being spoken though were Russian, a man's voice and a woman's.

As much as I wanted to see who I was looking at, I couldn't risk starting the car to use the wipers or even roll down the window. Quarrelling people are very similar to animals on the alert—any small movement or noise will distract them. I thought it would be better to let the argument run its course then see if I'd found the right woman.

The man stomped across the yard towards a dark-colored sedan parked in the driveway. His back was to me, but it looked like he was wearing a hat, like an English driving cap; the car was a four door and could have been dark blue, black or green.

He backed out and sped off, all under the eye of the woman in the doorway. Once the blurry taillights of the man's car had winked out around the block, she stepped back inside and threw the door shut.

I got out of my car hoping I wouldn't receive the same treatment as the guy before me, trotted through the rain up to the door, and rang the bell.

30

☐ I'd hit the bull's eye with my first throw. Sara's eyes went from slits of anger to wide-eyed surprise. "Expecting someone else?" I asked.

"How did you find me?"

"Never answer a question with a question," I said. "It makes people think you're hiding something."

"Well I certainly wasn't expecting you since I never offered an invitation. That should have been obvious," she said, folding her arms. The accent I'd heard being hurled out the door toward the retreating man was no longer present, not even a hint of it coming out with her annoyance. Sara's first language, I decided rather unscientifically, was probably English.

"True enough," I said. "May I come in, though? Or shall I just drive away like your last guest who you pushed out into the rain?"

Her face softened, and she looked past me to where the sedan had been parked in the driveway. She opened the door wider and stepped aside. I ducked into the warmth of the house and swept the water from my face and jacket.

The entryway reminded me of my own house. It was a small square alcove with just enough space for two people to stand and seemed to extend the front door away from the rest of the home with an archway.

Beyond the foyer was a tidy living room made all the more so by the lack of a television. A crimson sofa and two matching chairs surrounded a low, square coffee table like schoolyard bullies. The walls were white, decorated with large framed prints by Wyeth, Renoir, and a few I didn't recognize. Two floor-standing lamps by the furniture cast a warm glow into the room while the art was illuminated from above with halogen track lights.

Her living room was a lounge within a museum.

"So," Sara said, "how did you find me? And why? I thought we were through."

I walked past her and sat on the nearest chair without saying a word. My breach of etiquette offered a few moments of awkward silence, but she soon sat down across from me. "Well?" she said.

"I found you because I want to know what you're not telling me. Like the fact you speak Russian fluently." Many of the top-level chess players in the US were Russian immigrants, and I remembered Tony Druga's wife had told me Charlie and Sara met at a chess tournament. I didn't know if there was a connection, but it was a place to start.

Sara's face remained still, and I felt the heat of her eyes as they burned holes in me. But I didn't flinch. Superman would have been proud. "I'm not sure what you mean," she said. "Plenty of people speak more than one language."

"Of course," I said and let the Russian question drop for the moment, "but I think I could have figured out if Charlie was gambling or not, even if I am just an ex-cop. Meeting me was something you needed to do so you could decide to be concerned or not."

"Concerned with what, Mr. Gordon? I've done nothing wrong."

"You know what? I believe you. But I also think you're hiding something." When Sara didn't say anything, I asked, "What happened to Gregory anyway?"

What color there was in Sara's cheeks slid down like a sheet of ice falling from a glacier. The way she stared blankly into the space between us, I would have believed I'd killed her with those words except for the tears that welled up and rolled down her face.

"How did you find me, Mr. Gordon?" she asked quietly, her eyes still looking at nothing.

"County records. Sara P. Roggenbuck. I almost thought it couldn't be true."

She nodded to herself. "Charlie couldn't marry me, but I wanted our son to share his name. So I lied."

"What do you mean Charlie *couldn't* marry you?" I asked. She was staring at me, but she didn't see me. Her mind was in a different time. "Sara?" I said. "How did your son die?"

"I want you to leave now, Mr. Gordon."

"What happened to your son, Gregory?"

"He's not here."

Sara never said another word. I left her sitting in her chair, staring at her memories.

31

☐ By the next morning, the rain had gone but the clouds remained. Seattle was an artistic city and popped with fresh, often vibrant hues during the spring and summer, but when winter clouds blocked the light, the city was encased in gray like re-bar cast in cement.

I'd found Sara and gotten nowhere. Now I needed information about Charlie and his alleged gambling, and while I'd been on the mark with Sara P. Roggenbuck, I didn't think my luck would stretch much further. Tommy found Sam Scott at the Eagle's Nest Casino near Olympia. It was an hour drive, which gave me plenty of time to pay a visit to my alma mater first.

At the University of Washington security office I asked to see Louis Martin. When I was a cop, I busted Louis for the armed robbery of a liquor store. Technically, he wasn't armed, but he pretended to be by keeping his hand inside his jacket pocket. It sounded silly, but armed or not, the guy behind the counter wasn't going to take any chances with a guy who stood six-four and was built like a Greek myth. There were only a couple hundred bucks in the till, and Louis walked out without an argument.

The problem was, Louis didn't have someone outside as a lookout. I'd been ten steps behind Louis when he entered the liquor store. Whether he knew I was behind him or not, I don't know, but he never bothered to check his back before committing the crime.

I saw him go right up to the counter and start yelling at the cashier. Something was up, so I stood a few feet back from the door where I could see in without too much interior light falling on me.

When Louis came out, I slapped a cuff on his right wrist, pulled him toward me, and swept his feet out from under him. He hit the ground like a bomb. The element of surprise let me roll him over and cuff both hands behind his back before he could put up a fight. I told him he was under arrest, and before I could even start reading him his rights he threw up.

It turned out Louis Martin was trying to bail his mom out of debt. His father had died of cancer, and the medical bills had depleted the family savings. Then his mother got injured at work and was being held at arms length by their insurance company. In the meantime, the bills kept coming and mother and son stood to lose everything.

It was Louis's first offense, there was no weapon—though it didn't really make a difference—and the District Attorney let him off with community service in exchange for a guilty plea.

I actually felt sorry for Louis, and while I wasn't supposed to tell anyone, the D.A. did too. Louis Martin was a good kid driven to stupidity by desperation. But he'd done what he'd done and was labeled with a felony conviction for the rest of his life.

I pushed to help get Louis a job in security. Given that he was the size of a small rhinoceros, who wouldn't want him? Intimidation can be very effective. The D.A. dropped a couple names, and a week later Louis Martin was working security at the University of Washington.

I sat and read a National Geographic while I waited for Louis, but he appeared in the lobby before I could even start looking at the photographs.

"Officer Gordon," he said, shaking my hand. "To what do I owe this pleasure?"

"Louis, I'm not a cop anymore," I said.

He nodded sheepishly. "I know, but it's how I know you. Always will."

"Okay."

We got through the reticent chitchat about how we were doing, the weather, and what we'd been up to. Then I sprang it on him. "Louis, I need a favor," I said.

"Anything!" he said. "Of course!"

Kortnie's boyfriend, Derek Griffith, was like a boil on her skin. He would continue to fester unless he was removed. I wasn't going to beat him up, but I thought a decent threat would work well enough. Within three minutes of asking, Louis had the information I needed, and I was walking across campus. Derek Griffith would be out of class in about ten minutes.

I walked within a pack of students huddled against the weather with their heads down and their hands jammed into pockets. When I got outside the lecture hall, I sat down next to a girl who seemed to be waiting for her class and asked to borrow a piece of paper and a pen.

I wrote Derek's name on the page and gave her back the pen. "Thanks," I said.

"You're not a student are you?" she said, telling me a fact rather than asking a question.

"Is it obvious?" I asked.

"No books. No paper. A little older." She said the last one with a smile.

I smiled back. "You must have read Nancy Drew when you were growing up." She frowned in confusion and I said, "Or maybe not." Then the doors to the lecture hall burst open.

Students poured out like insects from a hive and the once quiet campus was buzzing with activity. I stood up and held the paper with Derek's name on it above my head like a limo driver looking for his pick-up.

I got plenty of looks, but no takers. One or two students looked at me as if I were some kind of crazy street cleric holding a sign admonishing their sins but they kept walking. Then I caught a guy glancing over his shoulder. I followed his line of sight and saw his friend holding back from the crowd. When the trailer's eyes and mine locked, he turned and bolted around the corner of the building.

I leapt down and pushed my way through the remaining stragglers and made it to the corner where Derek had vanished, but I was too late. The grassy area beyond was a sea of dull green dotted with patches of yellow and blanketed by students and faculty rushing to and from their classes. It had been a long time since my university days, and I couldn't remember the thin alleys between buildings and the hidden doors inside alcoves where Derek could get away from me. But I'd seen him. And he'd seen me.

After an hour on the road through sheets of rain and road-rage inducing talk radio programs, I pulled off the freeway and turned into a parking lot full of RV's, pickup trucks and mini vans. A towering sign, visible to drivers miles away, advertised "The Eagle's Nest Casino, More Slots! More Black Jack! More Winners!" in a brilliant merger of neon and electric light. The casino itself was decked out with cedar trim and was surrounded by evergreens and totem poles. It tried to blend in with the lush surroundings of the Pacific Northwest, but it looked big enough to house the Space Shuttle.

As soon as I walked through the glass doors I was lost in miles of computerized poker and slot machines neatly lined in rows, their microchips merrily binging and bonging in mechanized tones. A gray haze hung in the air and gave the place its own kind of smog fueled by the little smoke stacks hanging from the parched mouths of old ladies sitting in front of slot machines. Washington State had passed a law years ago that banned smoking in public places. The Indian Reservations somehow sidestepped the ruling, and the casinos became havens for people wanting to die of lung cancer.

I asked a passing waitress where I could find Sam Scott. She smiled, handed me a bottle of water, and told me to wait where I was. She'd go and get him.

Just when I realized I would have to buy new clothes to get out from under the nicotine smell, I noticed a man staring at me. He had a set jaw like he was mulling over an expense report, a tailored three-piece suit that was cut in Europe, maybe New York, and a foot-long ponytail pulling his hairline backward and giving his sun-browned forehead more room. He stepped in front of me and thrust out his hand. He could be nothing other than a casino manager.

"My name's Sam Scott," he said and smiled as if he'd been asked to. "I'm the manager here at the Eagle's Nest. How can I help you? Are you looking for a particular game?"

I shook his hand and wondered how much I could trust a man with two single-syllable first names. They were probably trophies, the names of the first two people he'd rubbed out. "I appreciate the welcome, Mr. Scott, but I'm not here to gamble. My name is Ray Gordon. I'm looking into a homicide."

"I see," he said. "Of course I'll help in any way I can."

"Is there somewhere a bit less active we can talk?" I asked, looking around at the flashing lights and chain-smoking geriatrics moving back and forth like zombies between slot machines and video poker.

Sam Scott's office was comfortable but not as garish as I guessed it would be. The walls were decorated with western-style paintings of wildlife along with a few Native American artifacts like baskets and peace pipes in glass cases. Not exactly the décor I expected from an ex-wise guy from New York. A huge Citizen Kane style desk squatted in front of a window opposite the door, and a dull gray safe that would have made Al Capone giddy engulfed one corner of the room.

"Now what can I do for you, Mr. Ray Gordon?" he asked, sitting in the leather chair behind the acre of smooth mahogany desktop.

"I've been told you knew Charlie Roggenbuck. Is that true?"

"Ah, yes. Charlie," he said thoughtfully. He leaned back in the chair and steepled his fingers. "I read about what happened to him in the paper. It's really too bad considering."

"Considering what?"

"That he was looking to move out here."

"I'm not following you," I said. "He was an internationally ranked chess player on the way to becoming the World Champion, not to mention his stake in a New York City restaurant, and he was planning to move *here*?"

"Not right here, Mr. Gordon," he said tapping the desk. "Actually I think he had his sights set on a place on Whidbey Island."

"How do you know all this?" I asked, my voice rising a bit. It was frustrating to think that if Charlie had visited me on his frequent trips to the area I might know more, might be able to help more. Instead, I was getting information about my friend from a casino jockey.

"Since you didn't show me a badge I take it you're not a policeman, right?" Sam Scott asked. I shook my head. "And you used to be a friend of Charlie's?"

"I thought I was."

"How'd you know him?"

"I thought I came here to ask the questions."

"Please. Indulge me."

I'd come to get information from Sam Scott. If he wanted to give it quid pro quo, so be it. "We met in college, over at U-Dub. Been friends ever since, saw each other on occasion at chess tournaments but we kind of lost touch the last few years."

Scott nodded and frowned dully like a philosophy professor. "So you know nothing of his life for the past few years," he said.

My hands shook slightly with the rush of anger that coursed through me. Why did this guy, out in the middle of the sticks, seem to know more about Charlie's life than I did? I had been a friend! What was Sam Scott to Charlie Roggenbuck?

I don't know if my anger showed, but Scott seemed to read my mind. He opened a drawer and withdrew a folder. "Charlie and I were dealing with each other on a business level," he said, putting the file down on the desk in front of him. Charlie's name was handwritten in black marker on the tab. "Over the last couple of months we'd talked about him wanting to do some investing."

He emphasized the word investing so I wouldn't take it in the traditional sense. Sam Scott was actually doing the investing since he would be the one receiving a profit. "Why would he need to *invest*?" I asked.

"It took a while, but just a few weeks ago I'd told him I wasn't sure if I was looking for any more investors. Between you and me, he seemed desperate, and I was concerned he might have a gambling problem."

"Meaning you were worried you wouldn't get your money back," I said. The way he kept using the analogy of investments, I wondered if he thought the Feds had bugged his office.

He smiled. "Anyway, when I told him that, he told me why he needed to invest."

"So he didn't have a gambling problem?"

"No. He didn't."

"So why did he need to *invest*?" I asked, sitting forward in my seat.

"He needed the money to find his son."

32

☐ "What do you mean 'find his son'?" I asked.

"I don't know the whole story, Mr. Gordon. Charlie told me his son had vanished…"

"Vanished? Wait a minute. I'd been told his and Sara's baby had died at birth."

"Charlie thought that as well," Scott said, "until not too long ago when he learned the boy had been given up for adoption. He wanted to get him back and needed a high dividend, quick-turnaround investment to get the money it would take to find him." He shrugged. "Simple as that."

"Simple? I doubt finding an adopted boy would be simple. What's it been, five or six years?"

"Which is exactly why he came to me."

"Mr. Scott," I said slowly, "I am not a police officer, and I have zero affiliation with any law enforcement agencies in this area. Is that perfectly clear?"

"Yes," Scott said, sitting forward and leaning on his desk.

"Good. All I want to do is find out who killed him. I'm certain it wasn't you, so any information you have can help. Understand?"

"Yes, I do, Mr. Gordon. But what makes you think I know more than what I've already told you?"

"Because from what I've been told, you and he were, how do I put this? Acquaintances. He confided in you at a time of desperation. People who do that tend to rattle off things they didn't intend to reveal." What I really wanted to know was why Charlie had not come to me? I had money and was someone he could trust.

Scott smiled thoughtfully. "You make it sound as if you think I'm doing something illegal here. I assure you, my casino is perfectly clean."

"I have no doubt," I said, not wanting our genteel conversation to head south, "and I certainly don't want to imply anything. But perhaps Charlie came to you for more than a quick turnaround on his investment. Perhaps you have connections, or you know someone who has connections that Charlie might have used to help with the recovery of his son. Possible?"

"Anything's possible, Mr. Gordon," he said with a smile. "I'm not from this area originally, so of course I know people in a few places. But like I said, I run a clean casino."

I nodded. "Understood."

"Good. Now, you seem a bit desperate yourself. How much have you learned about Charlie, and are you going to tell me the whole story?"

He was still deciding whether or not to help me. For every ping he gave me, I needed to deliver a pong. "The only thing I'm pretty sure about is Charlie's killer is one of the chess players at the US Championship. Call it a gut feeling since I still don't know why he was murdered. What I do know is the lead investigator wants to blame me because I found the body and Sara, the mother of Charlie's baby, isn't helping me. I can't tell if she's embarrassed about something or protecting secrets. And to be perfectly honest, I don't know why in hell Charlie confided in you instead of me." I couldn't help it. I felt wounded and saying it out loud was like a salve.

Scott nodded, apparently satisfied. "We knew each other in passing. Like you said, acquaintances more than friends. It's always easier to tell secrets to someone you don't know, even more so if there's something to be gained. Don't you think? He did it, and you're doing it now. But I also know he didn't come to you or anyone in the chess world because he was uncertain. You especially since you were close. He was ashamed."

There was nothing else for me to say. I wasn't sure if Sam Scott had just made my load lighter or heavier, but at least I had an answer. I nodded and kept my mouth shut.

"Now," Scott said, taking a slip of paper and a pen from their places on the desk, "on to possibilities." He wrote a phone number on the piece of paper and slid it across the desk. "Call this number in Seattle and ask for Chen."

"Thank you," I said, pushing the note into a pocket.

"Two things, Mr. Gordon. Use my name when they answer, and don't make him mad."

I nodded and we stood up together. "Thanks for your help," I said, shaking his hand.

"With what little time I knew him, I liked Charlie, too. I'm sure I'll read in the paper about your success finding his killer." He squeezed my hand a bit more, raised his eyebrows slightly, and lowered his chin. He looked like a mime but I got the message: no need to call again.

33

☐ The Hideout opened every day at eight a.m., except Sunday. On Sundays, the doors were unlocked at noon. Whether it was out of respect for the Sabbath or if it was because the guy with the keys slept late, I didn't know. It's just the way it was.

Good thing it wasn't Sunday, because I arrived at nine and set up one of my well-used sets of chess pieces on my vinyl roll-up board for my regular weekly game with Tommy. I ordered pastrami on rye and called his cell. No answer. By my watch he was only ten minutes late so I practiced my openings, moving pieces, countering and looking for other possibilities, all from memory.

When I'd finished my sandwich and he still hadn't shown, I was worried. Tommy called the night before from The Eagle's Nest Casino and said Sam Scott was spooked by him. To me, Sam Scott didn't come across as the type who would order a hit on someone just because he was nervous. Of course, there was a veiled kind of threat at our departure…

I called Tommy's cell again. After the fourth ring he answered. "Tommy? Where are you? Did you forget about our game?"

"Sorry, Ray," he said. "I just woke up. I'm in the hospital."

"What? What happened?" If he told me a casino security guard had shot him for harassing Sam Scott, the Knight odds deal for our next chess game would be nixed.

"I got ran off the road last night."

Just as bad, I thought. "Are you okay?"

"Banged up a bit but I'll survive. Bring your board over, and we'll play our game here. I have a story to tell you."

Alex still hadn't shown up at the Youth Center so in the hopes of spotting him, I drove along Elliott Bay on my way to see Tommy in the hospital. I took a left on Vine, then a right on 1st Avenue. It was still early and soggy enough to keep people off the street unless they had to be there. The thinned crowds made looking for Alex easier, but the cold, wet weather didn't help. Almost everyone was wearing a hat, a hood or holding an umbrella and looking at the sidewalk to avoid puddles.

Pike Place Market was quiet; the big red neon letters of the famous sign cut into the gray but evidently wasn't inviting enough. I took a left on Pike Street and slowly moved into the shopping district. As I approached 4th

Avenue, the light turned red, and I stopped as a small group of pedestrians stepped from the curb to cross the street. If it had been a sunny summer day I wouldn't have spotted him because he would have blended in with the rest of the crowd. On a miserably wet and depressingly gray morning though, Alex's shaggy blond mop bobbing above the black raincoats was pretty hard to miss.

I honked the horn twice and while the whole crowd looked, I only waved at Alex. His eyes got big like he just saw the school bully bearing down on him.

And then he ran.

He got across the street and then sprinted west on Pike, the way I'd just come. It certainly wasn't the reaction I expected, and I kept my eyes on him in the side view mirror until my light turned green.

I made a left on 4th, gunned it, and got up to Pine Street just as the light went from green to yellow. Pine's a one-way heading west and I kept my foot on the gas. The tires slid a bit on the wet pavement, but I stayed in the lane and checked the mirror for any flashing lights. I shot across 2nd Avenue and then slowed down. Alex may have been young, but he couldn't have kept up the pace he was running at for long.

I turned south on 1st Avenue and cruised, watching both sides of the street. There were plenty of places to hide: T-shirt shops, fast food restaurants, souvenir stores, and one or two mini-markets, but I didn't see Alex.

Then I saw a blond head duck into a record store.

After another fifty feet, I slid into an open parking slot and cut the engine. Why would Alex run from me like that? He must have done something illegal or gotten hooked up with the wrong bunch of kids or something. He was scared.

I got out of the Land Cruiser and trotted over to the record store. CD store. Whatever. They sold music. Once inside, I scanned the interior from my extreme left to right and saw him skimming over the hip-hop titles. There were only four other people in the store, including the Rastafarian wannabe behind the cash register, so it wouldn't be too long before he spotted me.

There were no other exits I could see and it was a small store. All I needed to do was keep Alex in front of me. The aisles were thin, but he might try to go around so I moved fast.

I wasn't sure what I was planning. Alex wasn't a criminal, and I was no longer a cop. All I really wanted to do was talk and find out what was going on with him.

"You can't do anything to me," he said when I was about five feet away.

"What do you mean?" I asked, glancing at the other customers. Had they heard his implied accusation?

"You know."

"No, I don't know. What's going on, Alex? Why'd you run when you saw me?"

He stopped perusing the CDs but kept his eyes locked on the row at waist level. "Just leave me alone, Ray," he said.

Alex had never called me by my first name. Even when we were first introduced, it was a laid back, though somewhat quiet, "Hey, Mr. Gordon."

"No, Alex. I won't leave you alone. Just tell me why you haven't been to the Youth Center. Mary's worried sick. When was the last time you were home? Are you in trouble?"

He rolled his eyes and snorted like I was incredibly naïve. He started to walk past me, but I stepped in his way. He stopped quickly and leaned back, unwilling to touch me, recoiling almost.

"Oh," I said, and realized what had happened. I'd seen other people react the same way when someone they knew or loved had been accused of a serious crime. "You think I did it, don't you?"

Alex took a step back but kept his eyes on the floor. "You're no better than my loser parents," he said. "Only you're rich and got a big shot lawyer."

It suddenly got very warm, and I took a step forward.

"Don't touch me," he said.

"Alex," I said, keeping my voice low, "how can you think that? Why would you think I killed my own friend?"

"The day you couldn't make it in, a couple of us went to Seattle Center, we figured you were there. They told us you were in jail, that the cops busted you for murder."

"Damn it, Alex," I said, shaking my head. I wanted to throttle him. "You need to get all the facts before you act. Now listen to me. The cop who arrested me is my ex-partner. I'll be honest with you. He's an ass. He only arrested me because I was the one who found Charlie's body. In his eyes that makes me a suspect. He's wrong. Okay? I promise you, I didn't kill anyone. Okay?" Nothing. "Alex? Look at me. Okay? I didn't do it."

He looked at me, his eyes heavy. He nodded and looked down again.

"You threw the brick through my window, didn't you?" I asked.

Pause. "Yeah."

"The graffiti on the back?"

A nod.

"My tires?"

"Yeah."

"Damn it, Alex!"

"Sorry."

"You almost killed Morphy!"

"What?"

"My dog. He's limping around like a mummy because his leg's all stitched up."

"Oh man."

"Alex…" I paused because I didn't want to ask, but I needed an answer. Too much had happened in a short time span. People had been killed, property had been vandalized, and both my dog and me had landed in the hospital. Who was guilty of what? "Alex, did you stab me?"

"What? You got stabbed?" His eyes were wide. "When? What happened?"

I smiled to myself. "Come on. I'll tell you about it on the way to the Youth Center. Then you can tell Mary what you've been up to. It'll make her feel better." I put my arm around his shoulders and steered him toward the door. "By the way, your mom needs smokes."

Harborview Medical Center engulfed several city blocks between James Street and Yesler Way near I-5. It was the same hospital I woke up in with a hole in my back two days earlier. I found Tommy's room, and since the door was open, went in.

He was sitting up in bed and had a white compress strapped to his forehead and his arm was in a sling. A doctor was standing next to the bed with his back to me. Tommy caught me coming into the room and said, "Hey, hey. There's Ray."

"Tommy Ryder," I returned confidently, sure he wouldn't carry out the joke in the company of the doctor. I was wrong.

"Ride 'er? I don't even know 'er!" he said.

The doctor laughed and turned to greet me. It was Dr. Clark, the physician/stand-up comic who'd looked after me. "That's good," he said. "I'm going to use that if you don't mind. Ah, Mr. Gordon. You two know each other? How are you healing up?"

"Not bad. It'll be a while though before I'm out playing soccer."

"Soccer?" he said. "I don't even know 'er!" He laughed and patted Tommy's bed. "Fantastic. I better be on my way."

Dr. Clark chuckled out the door, and I looked at Tommy. "Way to go. He'll be torturing people all day with that."

I sat down in a stiff faux-leather chair and said, "Okay, you got ran off the road. Do you know by who?"

"Wait, wait. Set up the board. I'll tell you all about it while we play. I'm actually feeling pretty good, considering."

I smiled. Tommy had never beaten me in a game of chess, but he loved it anyway. Losing never kept him from playing. I pulled the roll-around table between us, spread out the board, and set up the pieces so Tommy could play White. "What, are you feeling sorry for me so I get first move?" he asked.

"Something like that."

"Wait a minute. We agreed on Knight odds," he said.

I nodded and removed my Queenside Knight from the board, and he pushed out his King pawn. I mirrored his move, and the game was under way.

"All right," I said, "let's have it. What happened?"

"It was one of those big-ass logging trucks. Wasn't completely his fault though, I was trying to find a CD, almost hit him, and overcorrected."

"Sounds like it was all your fault," I said.

"He was crowding me."

"Hmm," I mused. "I hope you were at least looking for some decent music since it almost got you killed."

I brought out my lone Knight, and we hunched down, ready for battle. Before we spoke again, we'd each brought both Bishops into the game, his two Knights, and castled our Kings. A nurse breezed into the room to check Tommy's bandages and broke my concentration. "So that was the story you had to tell me?" I asked.

He brought a Rook up from the first rank and sat back in his bed so the nurse could examine him. He started to laugh and said, "I went over the side and ended up upside down in a mess of cedars and ferns."

The nurse and I looked at each other and she raised her eyebrows. "Why is that funny?" I asked.

"Because." He giggled. "It was pitch black out, I was down in the ditch, upside down and hidden by trees and plants and stuff. Somebody saw me go over, and the rescue team found me in no time because I painted the bottom of my truck orange! Remember? The emergency guys said every car company should do it as a safety feature. I need to patent it. I told you, I'm a genius!"

34

☐ A few years ago when Carla and I were on our way to a Husky football game, we were mired in the slog of traffic trying to get off the I-5. We were idling on the exit ramp when Carla pointed out the passenger window and said, "Is that guy...naked?"

I leaned forward and peered through her window. A series of two-story row houses lined the hillside opposite the I-5. The upper floors of each house had a rectangular deck that stuck out like a stiff lip and were peppered with ball-shaped barbecues, potted plants, fraying lawn chairs, and the occasional set of wind chimes. But directly across from us was a house with a completely unadorned deck except for a tall, oatmeal colored man, completely devoid of clothing. A steaming cup of coffee was on the rail to his left and his wanger was, thankfully, hidden behind a support post. His hair was pewter and a shade or two darker than the breath he exhaled into the crisp morning air. The naked man ignored the honks and hoots he received from the other cars waiting to exit the freeway, calmly sipped his coffee, and stared out into the cold morning.

When the traffic finally moved and we were able to limp forward by three car lengths, Carla looked again but he was gone, the naked man had disappeared inside his home and we never saw him again. The sad thing was I attended the University of Washington for four and a half years but the image I will have forever burned into my brain is the pale naked man, coffee at the ready, on a cold but sunny Seattle morning.

I looked out my passenger window as I slowed on the exit ramp that would ease me from the I-5 toward the U of W campus. The row house was the same color, the deck was still bare of décor, and the naked man was nowhere to be seen. But somewhere in the world of northwest academia lurked Derek Griffith. He'd gotten away from me once, but Louis had given me his class schedule for the week, and it was time for me to flush him out.

For some reason Derek had run from me, a person he did not know and who had simply held a sign with his name on it. I could have been from Publisher's Clearing House for all he knew, but instead he ran. Derek was into something bigger than slapping around his girlfriend. Whatever it was, I didn't care. If he was running dope or owed money or was just late for a job, I didn't care; it was none of my business. But he made it my business when he punched a certain young lady who loved my dog.

According to Kortnie, Derek fancied himself an athlete, and while he wasn't a member of any of the official UW teams, he spent quite a lot of time playing tennis. Most of the courts, fields, tracks, and sporting equipment were located on the southern end of campus and bordered Union Bay on Lake Washington.

I drove past Husky Stadium, parked on Montlake Boulevard near the Intramural Activities Building, and sat with the heater on. I watched students roam the sidewalks and lawns and figured someone would see me and call campus security soon. The sky was the color of an old quarter, and most of the students had their heads down to keep the chill at bay. Not too many had books; most were dressed in sweats or heavy coats. The street was empty, just a few parked cars, and occasionally a beat up pizza delivery truck would zip by. The buildings were hulking masses of brick and glass that watched everything silently as they dodged in and out of the fog coming off the water. It was mesmerizing, the rhythm of a college campus: Walkers, a jogger, silence, pizza delivery. Walkers, two joggers, die-hard cyclist, silence, pizza delivery. It was like bad poetry.

Somewhere in the middle of an iamb, I spotted a white hooded sweatshirt with Derek's head on top of it. He wore shiny purple polyester sweatpants and carried a pro-style duffel bag with three tennis racket handles poking out of it. He materialized from the fog by the basketball arena like a creature from the murky depths of the lake, but he strutted too much to be an inhabitant of the deep. He was just a punk with an attitude.

I got out of my car when he was within ten yards and said, "Derek, I'd like a word." He stopped and frowned at me, trying to place my face. Once he had it, his eyes widened slightly, and he turned and ran back the way he'd come. I slammed the car door shut and went after him. Derek was already ahead by fifteen yards, but I was gaining. It wasn't my extraordinary physique that let me close the gap, it was the duffel bag he refused to let go of. It was big and awkward and bounced against him like someone was running alongside and giving him a shove every few steps.

Derek disappeared around the corner of the basketball arena but when I reached the same point, I slammed into two guys coming toward me. They carried a couple of baseball bats, a bunch of balls, and a couple of mitts. Everything went flying when I struck them, and we all three landed on our asses. "What the hell, dude?" one of them sputtered. I ignored both of them and grabbed a baseball as I stood up. Derek had stopped to look when he heard the tangle of bodies behind him and stood less than twenty yards away with a victorious smirk on his face. When he saw me stand, he turned and started to jog away. I hurled the baseball from my best pitcher's stance and with all the juice I could muster. My back screamed, and I'm sure I yelped a bit as the stitches strained against my efforts, but my aim remained true. The ball hit Derek between and just below his shoulders, and he fell forward onto the ground like he'd just been struck from behind with a bat.

I grinned at the two young men who were still on the ground, but they didn't seem impressed. "Dude," the same one as before said. "What the hell?"

"Hold on," I said and trotted over to where Derek lay gasping for breath. I picked up the baseball and tossed it back to the boys and said, "Thanks." They picked up their equipment and rounded the building without another "dude", but it didn't mean they weren't about to call the cops. They'd just witnessed a guy assault a student for no apparent reason.

I looked down at Derek and rolled him over with my foot. He was a young man of maybe twenty-one to twenty-five, average height and build, maybe a little better looking than some of the other guys around, but nothing special. Black hair styled by someone who charged more than twelve bucks, blue eyes that weren't helped by contacts, and a nose to make a sculptor proud. There was something in the way he eyed me, though, like he was better than me and how dare I do anything to him. He was in shape but wasn't built like an athlete, so his self-assuredness had to come from something else. Money was my guess. I recognized myself at that age in him: cocky and confident—at least on the outside.

He sat up and coughed. "Okay," he said, folding his arms. "So?"

"What are you running from, Derek?" I asked.

"Look, man. I don't know you."

"Then why run? Am I scary?"

"What do you want? I didn't do anything."

"You put Kortnie Philips in the hospital. Now be nice and sit still, or I'll have you arrested for assault."

He kicked his duffel bag and backed up against a tree to face me and slumped down with a heavy sigh. "I didn't touch her," he said.

"Shut up. You know, I'll never understand why girls like her pick pinheaded jerks like you."

"Hey, man, I don't have to listen to this. Who are you anyway?"

"Someone who's going to trade favors with you. Here's the deal: You're going to apologize to Kortnie and then break up with her."

"What? No way!"

I shook my head. "You don't really get to negotiate, Derek. You end your relationship with her. Just tell her you met someone else and end it. Leave her alone. Got it?"

"So what do I get out of it?" he said.

"You stay out of jail. I'm an ex-cop, and I know plenty of guys on the job who would love to haul your sorry butt in and let you sit in a cell with some serious punks. Once they have you, they'll look into whatever you've been dealing."

He looked at me a little too quickly. "What's that supposed to mean? I'm not dealing anything."

"Did you hear what I just said, Derek? I'm an ex-cop. I know guys like you don't just run from a stranger because they think I'm going to offer them some candy and then kidnap them. You thought I was someone looking to collect something or break something, didn't you?"

Derek stared straight ahead and didn't say anything.

"You don't even like Kortnie that much, do you?" I asked.

"I don't know," he said.

"Just do it, Derek. I found you easily enough; I'll do it again. Understood?"

"Is that supposed to be a threat, Mr. Ex-cop?"

"Yes. Yes it is." I left Derek sitting at the base of his tree to contemplate his decisions in life and went back to my car.

35

☐ It was about time for lunch, so I went home and took Morphy out to the backyard for some personal time, made a mental note to buy some paint to cover up the graffiti, and then I loaded him and my laptop into the car and headed down to Red Mill Burgers. Morphy stayed in the car with his blanket and I took a bacon cheeseburger—without onions—out to him. I thought about holding the burger for him because if he dropped it on the floor, the big plastic cone surrounding his head would prevent him from retrieving it. He'd go mad. But I didn't need to worry; two bites and the burger vanished. So back inside I went and sat down at my computer.

The official website of the U.S. Chess Championship had a long official-looking letter explaining the cancellation of the tournament and what it meant for the world of professional chess. It also had a list of all the scheduled simultaneous exhibitions. All of them, except for Charlie's, were going to take place as planned. This was good because it meant at least ten players would be staying in Seattle another week. But it might prove to be irrelevant if Charlie's killer was, in fact, Ben Davis. He wasn't scheduled to play any simuls and he had vanished.

I went outside to check on Morphy. The car was still warm inside, and I gave him a handful of fries. My vet once told me I was going to love Morphy to death, but what was I supposed to do? Not share?

It was time to call the number Sam Scott had given me. I'd never called anyone in the mob or any sort of organized crime before, and I wondered if they had the ability to trace a phone call. I certainly didn't want any mobster hoods hanging around my favorite burger joint. Nearby there was a selection of phone booths to choose from—one at the gas station next door, two at the QFC grocery store across the street, and the one right next to me, attached to Red Mill Burgers at the base but leaning drunkenly away at the top.

So now I was about to buddy up with the criminal underworld. My best friend in the world, Morphy, looked like a giant flashlight on legs, and I was walking like a stiff zombie. We weren't in any kind of condition to effectively defend ourselves or each other should the meeting with Chen turn into some sort of goon-fest.

I walked over to the gas station phone booth, dropped a few quarters into the slot, and punched in the number Sam Scott had given me. After three rings the connection was made, but no one spoke.

"Hello?" I said.

"Source," said a gruff voice.

"What?"

"Name your source. Who gave you this number?"

"Sam Scott. I'm supposed to talk to Chen."

"Hold on."

I heard the phone on the other end being set down and footsteps on a wooden floor. Morphy was watching me from the front seat, and I waved to him.

"What?" another voice said in my ear.

"Is this Chen? I was told to call you and see if you might be able to help me with some information."

"Sam Scott gave you my number?"

"Yeah. And I'm not supposed to make you mad."

"Too late. I was eating."

"Sorry." I rolled my eyes.

"Whatever. You know the hammer man?"

"Yes."

"Meet me there in an hour."

"How will I know you?" I asked.

"Do you have gloves?"

"Yes."

"Wear the left one. I'll find you," he said, and the connection was broken.

I didn't really feel like I was putting myself in any real danger, but I also wasn't so naïve to think there was no possibility of Chen just shooting me dead since I'd interrupted his meal. I entertained the idea of calling Louis Martin, the University of Washington security guard, for a little back-up muscle, but I didn't want to appear either scared or too tough. Tommy Ryder could have been a lookout at the very least but he was nursing a broken arm. In the end, I decided to just go to the meeting with Chen alone but let someone besides Morphy know where I was.

Carla was the obvious person. Even though we weren't a couple, we were close. She was the only person who really knew me. But I didn't want to talk to her because then she'd worry and I needed my head on the right track. I shook my head. Dealing with the mob was making me crazy. Most likely Carla was at lunch with her artist friend and I'd get her voicemail, but I didn't want to risk it. Instead I called her mother.

"Mrs. Caplicki," I said when she answered. "Hi, it's Ray Gordon."

"Hello, Ray. Is everything all right?" Her voice had a slight tremble in it, a reflex I suppose, of having a friend of your child call when your child doesn't live at home anymore.

"Everything's fine, Mrs. Caplicki. I just need to leave a message for Carla." She was silent for a moment, and I felt like I was in junior high calling to see if her daughter liked me.

"Raymond, what's going on?"

"I know how weird this sounds, but I really need you to just hang up and let me leave a voicemail. I can't really risk talking to Carla right now. You can listen to it later, just don't erase it."

She sighed. "When are you going to stop playing games, Raymond? She can't wait for you forever."

The 'she' Mrs. Caplicki referred to, of course, was Carla, and I agreed. I'd been playing games and keeping her at arm's length for too long. Not games in the normal sense of the word when it comes to the relationships of men and women. I wasn't playing her along. If anything, I was fooling myself. Carla had always been there for me, been there for stupid high school dances and pep rallies, college football games and parties. My whole life, really. But it was my fear of losing someone again that kept me from igniting a true romance with her. "I know," I told Mrs. Caplicki. "No games. Remember what we talked about? I said I'd figure it out, and I have. Really. But I do need to leave this voicemail." It might be the last call I ever make, I thought.

"All right, Ray," she said, and I could tell she wore a smile. "But only because I like you, and I know you'll do what's right. I hope everything's okay."

"Me too," I said. "Talk to you later." She hung up, and I waited five seconds before redialing her number.

The hammer man was a sculpture at the front entrance of the Seattle Art Museum. It's a forty-eight-foot-tall silhouette of a man holding a hammer in his right hand. The arm is mechanized so it moves up and down, creating the illusion of a sculptor or a blacksmith swinging a hammer.

I sat on the edge of a planter box in the gathering darkness and tried to look like I was wearing one glove on purpose. First I sat with my arms crossed, but that hid my hands. Then I tried displaying my hands on my knees, but that looked too prim. Finally, I just clasped my hands in my lap and sighed. No one seemed to pay any attention, but I knew I was being watched. My question was, how long would I be made to wait?

It wasn't long. Something I'd always found amusing as a cop was how organized crime was so 'professional,' complete with courtesies and manners. Usually. Doors were opened for 'clients', men were addressed as Mr. or Sir, and tempers were held in check. After all, it was just business.

My wait was no longer than five minutes, enough time for Chen and whatever backup he'd brought to scope me out and canvass the area. He materialized from the crowd and sat next to me without looking at my face.

"I am Chen," he said with a slight Asian accent. "Why don't we go inside where it's warm?"

We crossed the few steps from the planter box and passed through the glass doors into the nearly unbearable heat of the museum's marble foyer. Both of us stripped off our coats—and I removed my left glove—and Chen led me to the ticket counter. After he had bought two tickets, we checked our coats and stepped through the metal detector. Neither of us set off any alarms, and once through I turned to him. "So you know I'm not armed?" I asked.

"And so you know that I am not either."

Chen was about five-six and built like a bulldog. His shoulders and biceps bulged his black T-shirt, and he walked with an air of readiness. His hair was black, spiky on top, long in back. A hint of crow's feet at his eyes led me to guess he was in his early thirties. I didn't think for one minute this man couldn't kill me with his bare hands if he wanted to.

Neither of us spoke as we started into the museum. I was not versed in thug etiquette, so I let him take the lead. He stopped and looked at a painting of a stone. The stone was as big as my fist and sat at the bottom corner of an eight by ten canvas. The rest of the canvas was white.

"What, exactly, do you want?" he said quietly.

"Don't you want to know my name?" I asked.

"I haven't decided if I will conduct business with you yet. No need for a name until I take the job."

I nodded. It sounded reasonable. "One of the chess players who was killed was my friend. It had been a long time since I'd seen him, but I've come to understand he was searching for his son. Are you familiar with any of this?"

Chen said nothing as he walked away from me and around a corner. When I caught up to him he was studying a sculpture from ancient China. "Charlie Roggenbuck worried too much about appearances," he said. "And I don't mean his physical appearance, although the man had no respect for his body. He was worried about how he would look to his colleagues when they discovered what had happened to his child. It drove him mad."

"How do you know this?" I asked, grabbing his arm and spinning him around. This was the second person to know more about Charlie Roggenbuck than he should have. He glanced at my hand, and I let go.

"Don't do that," he said. "Allowing your emotions to navigate your actions is a very costly mistake."

"Is that a threat?" I asked.

"Not at all. It's an observation. Emotions ruin people's lives all the time. It's precisely what happened to Mr. Roggenbuck."

"*What* happened to him?" I asked exasperated. Chen stared at me but remained silent. His obsidian eyes revealed nothing but a mirror image of myself. I threw my hands up and backed away from him. The green walls around us seemed to be moving inwards, the giant canvases of swirling color collapsing upon me. I blew out my breath and turned away. Was Chen a hit man or a philosopher? How was he involved with Charlie? Had he killed him?

"Let's sit down," Chen said, taking my elbow and steering me to a bench. We sat facing the heavy brush strokes of a Van Gogh. "What's your name?" he asked.

36

☐ I spent the better part of an hour in the Seattle Art Museum with Chen and came out without any more knowledge of the modernistic movement or the masters of cubism than I'd gone in with. But I had learned more about Charlie and why he was dealing with shady loan sharks and mercenaries for hire. Chen told me everything he knew without "taking the job" and because of that I owed him a favor, which made me wish I'd brought some Rolaids along.

I called Sara and told her of my conversation with Chen. I knew more, but only she could fill in the blanks I was left with.

"Mr. Gordon," she said, "I've worked to put this all behind me. Why do you insist on bringing it back up?"

"Sara, I need to know if this has anything to do with Charlie's murder. Only you can help me figure that out. I'm on my way over now."

It was dark and raining when I pulled into her driveway. It was just like the first night I'd been there and it is still how I remember her.

There was no answer when I knocked. Next I rattled the door with the heel of my fist and called her name. Nothing. I walked around to the garage to see if she'd ditched me and holed up in a motel somewhere, but the car was there.

I stepped into muddy flowerbeds to peek in the windows that surrounded the house, hoping the neighbors wouldn't take me for a peeping tom. At the kitchen window, I saw Sara's shadow in an adjoining room. The lights were on behind her, but the shadow she cast was odd. There was light where her feet should have been.

With a running start, I broke open the back door with my shoulder and landed against the small island in the middle of the kitchen. "Sara!" I called. No answer. I moved into the dining room where her shadow fell across the floor and found her hanging in another doorway. Her feet were a foot from the floor and a chair lay on its side inches away.

I backed across the room and kept my eyes toward the floor as I dialed the non-emergency number for the police. Keller was going to be pissed. When I hung up, I forced myself to look up at Sara again.

Her eyes opened.

"Jesus!" I didn't know if I was swearing or praying. Within two seconds, every creepy horror movie I'd ever seen flashed before me, but I found myself in the kitchen scrabbling through drawers with shaky hands. I grabbed the biggest knife I could find and ran back to Sara. I put my free arm around her waist and reached up with the knife to sever the bed sheet she'd wrapped around her neck.

We came down in a heap on the floor. I cut the sheet from her neck and called 9-1-1, all the while her eyes were open and panicky, but she never made a sound.

Sara shivered and shook uncontrollably, and her eyes were wild and unfocused. She looked confused, scared, and like she didn't really belong on this planet any more. All I could do was hold her hand. I didn't know if she was in pain or if she even knew I was with her. For an agonizing ten minutes we waited for the ambulance to arrive. When I finally saw the pulsing red lights in front of the house I reluctantly slipped away and let the paramedics in the front door. It hadn't occurred to me to tell them the back door was smashed open.

I stood in the corner and watched the medics check Sara's vital signs and do what they could to care for her. I lost track of time, and then Detectives Keller and Peters appeared in the doorway as the EMTs lifted Sara onto their gurney. "What's going on, Gordon?" Keller asked. "We got word you had another body."

"I thought she was dead," I said. "As soon as I called the station she opened her eyes."

Keller pointed to a chair and took a seat on the couch. I remained standing though and Detective Peters stood in the corner casting an eerie shadow against the ceiling. "Have a seat, Ray," John said.

"All right," I sighed. Under the circumstances, having a seat sounded about right.

"How's your knife wound?" he asked.

"Sore."

He nodded. "Okay. Tell me what the hell is going on here."

I really wanted a drink. It wasn't every day a dead body, or at least a body thought to be dead, opened its eyes and caused a severe case of the heebie-jeebies. I looked around, but it didn't seem like Sara stocked anything stronger than chardonnay.

"Ray?" John said. "We haven't got all night."

I nodded. Fine. No drink. "Charlie Roggenbuck and the woman who lives here had a son together," I said.

"So this is Roggenbuck's wife?" John asked.

"No. They never married. Different religious beliefs or just a deep-seated hatred of the father, I don't know for sure. I'm not entirely clear on all of it, but apparently Sara's father wasn't happy about the relationship. When she got pregnant and wasn't married, he somehow kept them apart and then told her the child would not be welcome in his family. She moved out here from back east while Charlie was at a chess tournament in Europe. Their baby was born and she gave it up for adoption, but told Charlie it had died."

"Why'd she tell him that?"

I shrugged and stared at the table. "Maybe it was easier for her to just be rid of all of it. Maybe to keep Charlie safe from her father."

"You're kidding, right?"

"Nope."

"So who's her father?" Peters boomed.

John shot him a sideways glance and I shrugged again. "That's why I'm here. I came over to find out just that. From what I understand, for as long as she could, she never even told Charlie who he was. He just found out a year or two ago. Apparently she didn't want to tell me either."

37

☐ I didn't sleep after coming home from Sara's house. I tried, but my night with the living dead kept playing over and over on the surface of my brain like waves lapping at the shore. I sat at the kitchen table and watched the hands of the clock.

Chen had given me all the details he'd received from Charlie, though Charlie hadn't told him the identity of Sara's father either. I couldn't understand why Charlie and Sara were protecting Grandpa since he wasn't exactly a role model father figure. Maybe they weren't protecting him but rather, protecting themselves somehow. After all, Sara refused to reveal the identity of her father to Charlie for years. But why?

Chen told me he'd accepted the job to search for Gregory, but he needed half of the money up front. Apparently, searching for a child who's been in the adoptive system demands a hefty fee, and Charlie was to have contacted Chen once he had the money, but he never did.

Once I learned the truth of their son and their relationship, I understood Sara's reluctance to discuss it. I wondered if she had readily agreed to give up her baby or, and it seemed more likely given what I'd heard, her father had coerced her to do it. Her reluctance to talk about it, her tears and her desperate attempt to be rid of it all made me think she hadn't done it willingly. I also believed Charlie wasn't the gambler or cold-shouldered prima donna everyone was making him out to be. He was going to hire Chen to find Gregory, but wanted to do it under the table because he was either ashamed of the situation or too proud to ask for legal help. Sam Scott said Charlie was looking to buy a place on Whidbey Island, which would have meant even more money than what it was going to take to find his son. Had Scott lied to me? Had a deal gone bad and they killed Charlie?

I flipped channels for an hour and wondered why I paid for cable TV. Finally, armed with a bag of potato chips and a six-pack, I prowled the Internet and played chess with faceless opponents until dawn. When the paper arrived, I read through it, noting no one I knew or needed to talk to had died—at least not that anyone knew about. After a shower and a quick breakfast, I called St. Nicholas Russian Orthodox Church and told Deacon Kamalov what had happened at Sara's.

"Yes, I know," he said.

"How do you know? It wasn't in the papers," I said.

"Late last night I got a call after she arrived at the hospital."

"From who?"

"He did not tell me his name, and I did not ask. I assumed he was a neighbor. I got there just in time."

"In time for what?"

"Her last rites. Didn't you know? There was too much loss of oxygen. She died soon after getting to the hospital."

"No. I didn't know."

"I'm sorry, Mr. Gordon."

I hung up and tossed the phone on the couch. What could have been so bad that Sara had killed herself over it? Did I push her over the edge? I knew I was digging in dangerous territory by asking questions about a suicide. I certainly didn't want another death on my hands. The guy I'd shot when I was a cop was an accident, but Sara had a choice. That's what I needed to believe, that I didn't kill her.

The back door to Sara's house was probably still open. What I had to do was go back and search for any evidence of her father: a letter, photograph, anything. There had to be something there. I checked my front door for taped-up messages, found none and then went and got in the car.

The drive across Seattle was mesmerizing. The evening rain had turned to a drippy fog. Faces emerged and then vanished with the bow of a head, the opening of an umbrella or the rush of a delivery truck. I saw them. I didn't see them.

When I finally turned into Sara's neighborhood, I could see from a block away my opponent was one step ahead of me. Sara's house was nothing more than some charred walls trying to stand straight. Blackened two-by-fours stood stark against the gray sky like skeletons.

A red fire marshal's car was parked at the curb, and I pulled to a stop behind it. The marshal and I both got out of our cars and leaned on them, he on the trunk of his, I on the hood of mine.

"Can I help you with something?" he asked.

"I'm investigating a homicide. The woman who lived here was involved in one way or another, and she committed suicide last night. Can you tell me how and when the fire happened?"

"Are you a cop?"

"Used to be."

He nodded. "Thought so. Gordon, right?"

"That's me." He looked at me and didn't say anything. He was probably trying to remember the whole media event that surrounded my leaving the force. The public services like police and firefighters had all had their credibility questioned by the media because of me, and while most were on my side, some held a grudge against me for creating such a mess.

"Where are the actual cops?" he asked.

"I'm sure they'll be along soon. You know Detective Keller out of the West Precinct?"

"Yeah, I've heard of him."

"It's his case."

"Well," the marshal said slowly, "it was definitely arson. Poured gas all over the house and set it off with a bomb."

"A bomb?"

"Yeah. None of the neighbors saw it, but they all heard it, and a few of them lost some windows and dishes." He looked at the houses up and down the street and shook his head. "I've never understood why people hang plates on their walls."

"What kind of bomb?" I asked.

"Homemade job. We found evidence of maybe five or six gas cans blown to bits in the living room."

I pushed off my car, walked to the nearest tire and kicked it. "No witnesses, right?" I asked.

"Never are. Happened about three in the morning. Was she pertinent to the case?"

"Yeah. Somehow. I only knew her by her first name. I came over this morning to see if I could scrounge something up."

"Nothing left in there," he said. "But this might help you." He ducked into his car and emerged with a clipboard. A fan of papers struggled against the spring clamp on top as he handed it to me. "That's the name on the deed," he said, pointing at the top line of his report.

I read it out loud. "Sara. Miranda. Penski."

38

☐ Of course it made perfect sense once I saw the name. Vladimir Penski and Charlie Roggenbuck were different in every aspect of their lives. Vladimir was old school Russian, a former soldier who grew up under the thumb of the Soviet Union, while Charlie was the young American consumed by fast food, movies, and got anything he wanted. Even their styles of play on the chessboard were different. Penski was slow, he controlled and manipulated the pieces into the game he wanted to play. Roggenbuck was an all out attacker with a never-say-die approach.

I couldn't help thinking, though, that they had Sara in common. What was it about Vladimir Penski that made Sara unwilling to even let him know who she was in love with? What power did he wield over his daughter that made her give up her child? Could sacrifices like those be justified?

Vladimir Penski was staying at the Sheraton Hotel—the same place Elena Johnson had met her fate, but he was gone.

"Gone, gone?" I asked the desk clerk when I called, "or just not answering his phone?"

"Mr. Penski checked out earlier this morning," the voice said politely.

"Thank you," I said.

I was driving north on Broadway when my brain finally started working and caught up with all the information I'd received over the past seventy-two hours. I hit the brakes and skidded into a parking slot in front of a Starbucks.

Vladimir was the man I'd seen coming out of Sara's house that rainy night. She'd been upset, lost almost, when I'd talked to her. They'd probably talked about Charlie's death, maybe he told Sara she was better off without him. They had argued, and she threw him out.

But not before he left something with her. Did Vladimir have something that implicated Ben Davis in Charlie's murder? Vladimir had been playing professional chess since before I'd started getting serious about it. He knew the players; he knew their rhythms, moods and personalities. It was possible Vladimir either knew or had physical evidence of Ben's guilt. And Davis must have known, followed Vladimir to Sara's house and was watching when she was taken to the hospital. He went in, probably didn't find what he wanted, so he destroyed the house rather than let whatever it was he was looking for be discovered later.

I dialed John Keller's cell phone number. "John," I said when he answered, "you need to find a guy by the name of Vladimir Penski. He's one of the chess players at the Championship. You have his picture in the stack of photos I gave you. I think he may have proof of who killed Charlie. Okay? Did you get that?"

"Yeah, I got it," he said. "Ray, where are you at right now?"

"Over on Broadway, up on Capitol Hill. Why?"

"We already have your boy, Penski, holed up, and he wants to talk to you. He's not giving us anything, just says he wants to talk to you."

"Okay. Where are you?"

"Your house."

39

☐ The scene outside my home was nothing short of a Hollywood movie set. I parked a block away and jogged into the array of flashing blue and red lights, police cars parked at odd angles in the street, uniformed cops with handguns drawn and trained on my front door and neighbors peeking out from curtained windows.

Kortnie Philips was sitting on the curb across the street from my house holding her knees to her chin. She ran and hugged me, her eyes scared and teary. "Oh Ray!" she almost cried. "I'm so glad you're not in there! I was so scared!"

"It's okay, Kort. I have to go talk to the police."

She leapt on me and attached herself with another hug. My knees buckled from the surge of pain in my back, but I stayed up. "Did you say something to Derek?" she asked.

I was looking over her shoulder at all the cops who were waiting. "I can't talk about it right now," I said.

"It's okay," she whispered. "Doesn't matter now anyway." She released her constricting embrace and looked at me. "Thank you," she said.

I smiled at her and then a uniformed officer urged her backwards. He turned to me and said, "You need to come with me, Mr. Gordon."

He brought me to my front curb where Keller was standing behind two police cruisers parked nose to nose and angled like a V. "What is all this?" I asked John and waved my hand at the mass of law enforcement clogging the street.

"I got a call from this guy saying he was at the house we were in last night. You know, where you found the woman? Then he tells me he's inside your house. I figured he was the one who torched it and was going to kill you and then light up your place too. Didn't find out you weren't in there until we got here. So who is this guy?"

I told John everything I knew and everything I thought I knew, while his partner, Detective Mark Peters, took notes.

"Your theory is good except for one thing," John said. "We know where Ben Davis is."

"Where?" I asked.

"New Mexico," Peters said. He flipped back a couple of pages in his notebook. "Right before the chess game with Elena Johnson he got a phone call from his boss. Cut backs. He got laid off."

Keller shook his head. "They told him over the phone while he was on vacation. He withdrew from the tournament and headed to the airport. We finally got one of his neighbors to go over to his house. You might say Mr. Davis is distraught, but he has a solid alibi."

I huddled out of the wind against one of the cars and thought about it out loud. "How does Elena Johnson fit into all of this? Did she kill Charlie, maybe out of jealousy? Had they been lovers at one time?"

"Maybe this Sara woman killed her out of revenge?" John asked when I finished.

I nodded. "Possible."

"What about you?" Peters asked. "You said a man attacked you."

True, I thought. "Maybe Vladimir knew Sara had committed the murder and did it to protect her. He put me in the hospital so I wouldn't find out."

"Why not just kill you?" John asked.

I wondered the same thing. "I don't think Vladimir is a bad person overall," I said. "Just an overbearing, overprotective father with an overdeveloped patriarch complex."

John snorted. "If what you say turns out to be true," he said, "my guess is a shrink will find him to be certifiable. It sounds like his daughter hated him and killed herself because of him."

"I mean in general. We're friends. It's probably why he came here now."

"Maybe we should find out," John said. He slid his thumb over his cell phone and then punched in a number. My number. After a few seconds he said, "Ray Gordon is here." Then he handed me the phone.

"Hello?" I said.

"Hello, Raymond. Do you know who this is?"

I nodded. "Yes. How are you doing, Vladimir?" My old police skills seeped into my voice, and I found myself speaking slowly, deliberately, and with care to a man who was on the edge.

"I am okay. Well, no, not so good. My daughter is dead. You know this?"

"Yes. I'm sorry about that, Vladimir. I really am. Is that what you wanted to talk to me about?"

"No," he said quickly. "No. It is done. Please come inside now. What I want to tell you is not for over the phone."

I hesitated. "He wants me to go inside," I whispered to John.

John shook his head slowly and whispered, "No way."

"Do you have a bomb in there, Vladimir?" I asked into the phone.

"No, Raymond. Why would I have a bomb? No more need for anyone to get hurt. It's all over."

"Okay," I said. "I'll come in the front door." We both disconnected, and I handed the phone back to Keller.

"You're not going in there," John said. "It's bad enough he's holed up in there and won't let anyone in. Who knows what he's got planned?"

"His daughter is dead, John," I said, "and he knows who killed Charlie. He's been under a lot of pressure. I'm sure he just wants to talk."

"Don't turn this into a hostage situation, Ray."

"He already has a hostage," I said, stepping between the cars and onto my lawn.

"Who?" John asked.

"My dog."

I turned and faced my house, and my senses became acutely aware of what was in front of me. The siding was still in good shape, but I could see a couple of spots that could use some sanding and a new coat of stain. The windows might need replacing too. The air bit at my skin, and the police radios squawked behind me.

Inside the house was a man I respected and admired. I'd improved my chess game by watching and studying his games, and I enjoyed his company at tournaments. So why were my hands shaking? Why was my heart dancing to a speed-metal beat? What was I thinking about as I trudged up my weather beaten lawn?

Carla Caplicki.

I about-faced, trotted back to the street and handed my phone to Mark Peters. "Call Carla for me, will you? She's the girl who was with me at Charlie Roggenbuck's hotel room. You have her number in your notes somewhere, but she's on my speed dial. Number one. Tell her what's going on and that I still want to talk to her. Can you do that for me?"

Peters nodded, took my phone, and started flipping the pages of his notebook backward as I retraced my steps toward the house.

Vladimir Penski was a man ready to snap. A lot had happened over the last few days, and he'd bottled up what he knew about it, let it percolate, and now he wanted to talk. To me. Why?

I stepped through my own front door as it was opened from inside. It was then that I realized why my heart was pounding. But it was too late.

40

☐ Vladimir motioned me to a seat after he shut the door. He held a snub-nosed .38 comfortably but lazily in his right hand and waved at my sofa with it.

"Where's my dog?" I asked and sat down.

"I closed him up in your bedroom," Vladimir said, looking toward the hallway. "He wouldn't stop licking me. And the cone around his head kept scraping my arm."

I nodded and smiled, then looked at the gun. "I thought you said no more. If that's true then what's that for?" I pointed at his pistol.

"It's for them," he said, pointing to the window. "Police only listen if there is possibility of violence."

"Okay," I said. "Well you've got me here. Why do you want to talk to me?"

Vladimir turned and went into the kitchen. "Coffee?" he called.

"Sure," I answered.

I heard him pour two cups and when he returned, the .38 was tucked into the waistband of his trousers. "Raymond," he said, "I've done some bad things in my life."

"That's not a great way to begin a conversation, Vladimir," I said. "How about you start by telling me why your coffee is so much better than mine?"

He smiled and shook his head. "Coffee is just coffee. We worry too much about little things like that in America, I think."

"What do you worry about?" I asked.

He stood and walked over to the chessboard where I had Charlie's last game set up, right down to the tipped-over King. "Who are you playing?" he asked.

"No one. Just analysis." My gut told me I was having a casual conversation with the murderer of Charlie Roggenbuck. It was my need to see Carla before coming into the house that did it. The pull that made me realize I needed her in my life as more than a friend had to have been the same for Charlie and Sara. They must have been together here at the US Championship and Vladimir finally discovered who'd fathered his grandchild. After years of boiling rage for something only he was upset about, he must have exploded.

"Looks like White can win enough material to take the game," he said. "Why did he resign?"

"He didn't," I said. "It was never finished. It's a game a friend of ours was playing."

Vladimir stared at me. His eyes widened, and his skin turned a shade of crimson. "Charles?"

I nodded. "What happened?" I asked.

Vladimir moved the pieces and set them up for a new game. "Let us talk over a game between friends," he said.

Since it was my house, Vladimir offered the White pieces and therefore the first move, to me. We sat and played through the opening moves and drank our coffee before he said anything.

After the twelfth move, he sat back, sighed and began to unravel the details for me. "I couldn't stand the very thought of Charlie once I found out it was he who ruined my daughter's life."

"How did you find out?" I asked. I wanted to tell him he was the one who'd ruined her life, but he was already stressed out—that and he had a gun.

"Sara told him I was her father. He came and informed me he was the father of her son and that it was *my* fault they weren't a family. He said he was going to find their baby, marry Sara and make sure I never saw any of them again."

"What happened?"

"I couldn't allow that to happen," he said. "Sara is all the family I have left." He stopped and looked at the board. "Had," he whispered.

"So you got a gun and killed him."

He nodded. "I waited for Mr. Brooks to leave and then went in."

"Did he say anything?"

"The door was open. I didn't give him the chance to say anything."

I felt hollow and sick. How could he just walk in and murder somebody in cold blood?

"How is your back?" he asked suddenly.

How do you answer a question like that? The guy had stabbed me in the back. Literally. "Better," I said.

"I am sorry about that. I like you, Raymond. I did not want to hurt you, but you were too close to finding me out."

I nodded. At least he didn't kill me, which was something. "What about Elena Johnson?" I asked. "How was she involved in all of this?"

Vladimir took a sip of coffee. "Greed," he said. "She knew Charlie and Mr. Brooks were playing outside of the tournament. Unfortunately, she chose the same day as I did to catch them in the act. I believe she was afraid of not being able to beat him at chess. She thought if she turned him in to the arbiters, he would be disqualified from the Championship. Instead, she saw me leave. She went into Charlie's room after I left, saw what I had done and decided to collect her winnings from me. Obviously, I couldn't let her be the keeper of my secret. I would lose my business and be bankrupt. How could I trust her?"

I sat back from the table and looked at him. His bushy eyebrows were bunched together as he scowled at the thoughts I saw churning on his face.

"Why, Vladimir?" I asked. "Why was Sara afraid to even let you know she had fallen in love with Charlie?"

"Family is the most important thing in life," he said. "My family is from Russia. We are an old family. Traditional. If I let Sara marry someone like Charles, we would have lost that; we would no longer be Russian. She would have lost her ties with her family, and her children would have none of it."

"You lost her anyway didn't you," I said. "You held on too tight, and now she's gone. Was it worth it?"

"Everything I had," he said as he placed a Rook on another square, "my Sara, my grandson, even Charles, is gone. I have no family because I was a stupid, angry old man."

Finally he said something I agreed with. "Did you blow up Sara's house?"

He nodded. "It was an accident. It was just supposed to burn, not explode."

"Why even do that?" I asked. "What did she have that you needed to destroy?"

He sighed and looked at the ceiling. "I was ashamed of her for what she did. I wanted to just erase it all. I was wrong. About all of it. I am sorry, but it is too late."

"So what are you going to do now?" I countered his Rook by pushing a pawn.

"Ah," Vladimir said. "We are at the end of our game. You see?" He moved his finger over the board pointing at pieces and tracing their future moves through the air. "You will be checkmated in six moves."

"Nice," I said. "I knew you were up to something after the Queen sacrifice, but I couldn't see it." Actually I had hardly been paying attention to the game.

He smiled, baring those horrible teeth, and stood up. "You see it all now, though. You are a good player, Raymond. Thank you for the game. It is nice to play a friend on occasion, just for fun. Don't you think?"

"I do," I agreed.

"Now I will go out and talk with the police." Vladimir turned and was out the door before I realized he had pulled the pistol out of his pants. It only took about a quarter of a second for the rage to boil up inside of me. Vladimir had murdered my friend, killed Elena Johnson, was the root cause of Sara's problems, had been the catalyst of Alex's loss of trust in me—and he wanted an easy way out of it all.

I leapt from my chair and charged out the front door just as Keller was yelling at Penski to lower his weapon. I dropped my shoulder and rammed Vladimir in the back. The blow knocked him forward, and we both flew out over the concrete steps like a couple of crash test dummies. He landed face first on my sidewalk, and I came down on his back. I heard a crack, like a stick being snapped in two, and Vladimir shrieked.

I rolled off of him and pushed the .38 he'd been carrying onto the lawn. The police quickly surrounded us, guns drawn, and cuffed Vladimir's hands behind his back. He barked something in Russian, and I told Keller that I thought I heard Vladimir's collarbone break.

"I'm sure it did," he said. "We heard it from over there."

I watched two uniformed cops hoist Vladimir to his feet and walk him out to the street where EMTs were waiting.

"Can you tell me what's going on here, Ray?" Keller said. "Why did he come out ready to have a gun battle?"

"He killed Charlie and Elena Johnson," I said and sat up. "He told me everything and then started whining about how he was all alone." I shook my head. "He came out so you'd shoot him and put him out of his misery. I thought that was too easy for him. All this time I thought it was Ben Davis. I didn't realize it was Vladimir until I walked inside."

"You okay?" Detective Peters asked from behind me. "You're bleeding."

"I think I popped my stitches. Hey, did you call Carla?"

"Yeah. She's right over there." I looked to where he was pointing and saw Carla. She was on her tiptoes looking over the top of a squad car. I waved her over as Peters helped me to my feet.

She ran over and hugged me. "Ray, are you okay? What happened?"

"Detective!" A voice called from inside the house.

Keller looked at me while he holstered his 9mm. I shrugged with one shoulder, kept a hand around Carla's waist, and we all went back in the house and into the kitchen. A uniformed cop pointed at an envelope propped against the coffee maker. *Police* was printed on the front.

Detective Keller looked at me again, and I shook my head. He opened it and read the handwritten letter inside.

"What is it?" I asked.

"A confession. You were right." Keller folded the letter, put it back in the envelope, and handed it to Detective Peters, who placed it in a brown paper bag. "When did he write this?" Keller asked.

I shook my head. "I have no idea. Must have been before I got here because I've been with him since I came in."

"Guess he wanted to clear his conscience before he checked out," Keller said. "What are you, a priest now?"

"Wow, I've never been called that before."

"Okay, boys," Keller said to the policemen, "let's pack it up."

Carla and I watched them troop out of the house and then liberated Morphy from my room. The cone around his head collided with the doorframe as he hobbled out as fast as he could, and he bounced like a pinball from one side of the hallway to the other in his joy to see Carla and me.

We sat in the living room and Morphy sat so she could pet him. "Poor Morph," Carla said. She rubbed his neck, scratched his ears, and lightly touched the bandages wrapped around his leg. "Do you remember calling me from the hospital?" she asked quietly.

I scrunched up my face and blew out air. I *am* ready for this, I thought. "Did I really? What did I say?"

"You said you wanted to talk about something. It sounded kind of important. Did it have anything to do with the message you left at my mother's?"

"Did you already listen to that?" I asked. When I called and left the message with Carla's mom, I thought it was entirely possible I'd end up dead in an alley somewhere, and I didn't want Carla to wonder about my feelings for her. On the recording, I thanked her for always being there for me. I told her what a fool I'd been and that I hoped she'd forgive me for keeping her at arms length for so long.

"Yes, I did," she said.

"And? What did you think?"

"Well, what exactly does it mean?" She smiled, and I thought I heard a catch in her voice.

I went and sat down next to her and took a deep breath. "I'd like to ask you out. On a real date. Complete with flowers, dinner, and a good night kiss."

"Oh? And where would this date be?"

"How about dinner at Mickey's?"

She smiled. "Why Mr. Gordon, I didn't know you cared."

"I do," I whispered. "I really do."

"Do I have to wait for the good night kiss?"

I smiled and my heart skipped. "Nope."

AUTHOR'S NOTE

The game Charlie was playing at the time of his death, is a real game played between Grandmasters Mikhail Tal and Robert Fischer in 1959. I borrowed this game from the book, *Twelve Great Chess Players and Their Best Games* by Irving Chernev (Dover, 1995; originally published by Oxford University Press, 1976). Since I paraphrased the expert annotations by Mr. Chernev for the use of this novel, any mistakes or miscalculations are purely my own. The entire game between Tal and Fischer is as follows:

White, M. Tal — Black, R. Fischer
Zagreb, 1959

1. d4	Nf6	18. exf5	gxf5
2. c4	g6	19. f4!	exf4
3. Nc3	Bg7	20. Qxf4	dxc5
4. e4	d6	21. Bd3!	cxb4
5. Be2	O-O	22. Rae1	Qf6
6. Nf3	e5	23. Re6!	Qxc3
7. d5	Nbd7	24. Bxf5+	Rxf5
8. Bg5	h6	25. Qxf5+	Kh8
9. Bh4	a6	26. Rf3	Qb2
10. O-O	Qe8	27. Re8!	Ndf6
11. Nd2	Nh7	28. Qxf6+	Qxf6
12. b4	Bf6	29. Rxf6	Kg7
13. Bxf6	Nhxf6	30. Rff8	Ne7
14. Nb3	Qe7	31. Na5!	h5
15. Qd2	Kh7	32. h4	Rb8
16. Qe3	Ng8	33. Nc3	b5
17. c5!	f5	34. Ne5	Resigns

The correspondence game between Ray and Simon is a real game played during the first World Correspondence Chess Championship in 1953. The game was played between Cecil Purdy, who went on to win the championship, and Mario Napolitano. I borrowed this game from the book, *The Search for Chess Perfection II* (Thinkers' Press, 2006). Again, any miscalculations or mistakes are purely my own. The entire game between Purdy and Napolitano is as follows:

White, CJS Purdy — Black, M. Napolitano
World Correspondence Chess Championship, 1953

1. c4	Nf6	24. a4	Nxf5
2. d4	e6	25. a5	h3
3. Nc3	Bb4	26. a6	Ra8
4. a3	Bxc3+	27. Bc5	Rfe8
5. bxc3	c5	28. a7	e4!
6. e3	Nc6	29. Rb7	Nh4
7. Bd3	e5	30. Qb3	Qf5!
8. Ne2	d6	31.Rdd7!	Nf3+!!?
9. e4	Nh5	32. gxf3	exf3
10. O-O	g5	33. Kf1!	Qxc5
11. Bc2	Nf4	34. Qc3!	Rf8
12. Ba4	Bd7	35. Qd3	Qe5!
13. Ng3	cxd4	36. Qxf3	Rae8!
14. Bxc6	bxc6	37. Rb1	Qxh2
15. cxd4	Qf6	38. Rb3	Qe5
16. Be3	h5!	39. Qxh3	Qf4!
17. dxe5	dxe5	40. c5!!	Qc4+
18. Rb1	Rd8	41. Kg2	Re4
19. Qc2	h4	42. Qf5	Qxb3
20. Nf5	Bxf5	43. Qxe4	Kg7
21. exf5	O-O!	44. Qf5	g4
22. Rfd1	Nh5	45. Qxg4+	Resigns
23. Bxa7	Ng7